"Livy, sweetheart."
hand

He drew tingly little circles on her palm. "We have to straighten out some things. Please have dinner with me."

Olivia jerked her hand away. "When hell freezes over! I will not—and read my lips if you're having trouble grasping this concept—I will not have an affair with a married man!"

Oops, that must have come out a little louder than she expected. Several heads turned in their direction. Good grief! The infamous Port Serenity grapevine would spread that one within hours, if not minutes.

Attention apparently didn't bother the good sheriff, because he simply smiled—and what a smile he had. Ooh, boy! Maintaining her immunity to the guy would take a resolve of steel, but Olivia intended to do exactly that. One broken heart was plenty, thank you.

"That's funny, I thought I said dinner." C.J. shrugged and put on his best cat-in-the-creamery expression. "But an affair sounds good to me." He paused for effect. "And let me make something perfectly clear. I'm *not* married."

Dear Reader,

Sheriff C. J. Baker and Dr. Olivia Alvarado welcome you back to Port Serenity, Texas, where life is never dull and romance blooms in the midst of murder, mayhem and well-meaning but ditzy relatives. (You may have met them in my first American Romance novel, *A Texas State of Mind*.)

For one blinding, rhapsodic moment, Livy fell head over heels in love with the sexiest sheriff on the Gulf Coast, but then she found out he was married. Supposedly it was all platonic—his way of helping someone out of a bad situation. Yeah, right. Okay, he *is* divorced, but Olivia has this itsy-bitsy problem with trust.... Getting jilted at the altar a decade ago tends to do that to a girl.

C.J. blew it—boy, did he blow it. Courting Olivia will be tough, but failure isn't an option. She's the best thing that ever happened to him. All rules go by the wayside in a skirmish of the heart.

Interspersed with their romantic sparring, Olivia and C.J. have professional encounters, too—a couple of dead bodies, an attempted kidnapping and an assault at the Super Saver. And this used to be such a quiet place! Add into the equation the rash of burglaries and the nefarious new citizens complicating life in their little haven of art galleries and Victorian B and B's, and you have the wild and wacky world of Port Serenity—C.J. and Olivia style.

So put your feet up, grab a glass of iced tea and enjoy another visit to the Texas Gulf Coast.

Ann

P.S. I love to hear from readers. My snail mail address is P.O. Box 97313, Tacoma, WA 98497, and my e-mail address is ann@anndefee.com.

TEXAS BORN
Ann DeFee

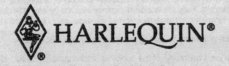

HARLEQUIN®

TORONTO • NEW YORK • LONDON
AMSTERDAM • PARIS • SYDNEY • HAMBURG
STOCKHOLM • ATHENS • TOKYO • MILAN • MADRID
PRAGUE • WARSAW • BUDAPEST • AUCKLAND

ISBN 0-373-75119-2

TEXAS BORN

To Bob—my husband, lover and best friend since we were children. Your support helped make this dream come true.

Chapter One

"Hey there, sweetheart. Mind if I join you?"

Dr. Olivia Alvarado switched her attention from her salad to the handsome man with the shaggy sun-kissed hair, mile-deep dimples and sea-green eyes that twinkled with humor and mischief.

"As a matter of fact, I do." She slammed her hands on the table. "I don't think my shots are current," Olivia hissed. "So get lost!"

She really didn't expect her unwanted visitor to take a hike; after all, the man's head was as hard as a granite slab. But she did harbor a slight hope that he'd accede to the southern manners his mama had tried to thump into his cranium and find his own table.

Instead of skedaddling, he responded with the boyish grin that had probably stopped girls' hearts all over south Texas. No! No! No way! Once burned, twice shy. And from experience, Olivia knew that this guy was capable of breaking her heart.

Daisy's Diner wasn't full—there were tables everywhere—so why did he want to sit with her? "I'm serious. Go someplace else for your caffeine. I hear they changed the coffee grounds at the courthouse," she muttered.

Sheriff C. J. Baker chuckled as he sat down on the vinyl bench next to her and scooted over so close his thigh was right against hers. "Sorry, can't do that. I want to talk to you."

Olivia moved toward the window and dredged up her best deep-freeze attitude. "Unless it's in regard to my official capacity as county coroner, I have absolutely nothing to say to you." She put on a saccharine-sweet smile. "But maybe I need to speak slower for you to understand. *Get lost*." Olivia drew out the short command into a polysyllabic order and turned her head.

There was a repeat of that irritating chuckle. "Trust me, I've gotten the picture. You won't answer your phone, you've ignored my e-mails, and believe it or not, I spotted you when you ran into the tax assessor's office. Darlin', my mama didn't raise a dummy. I know avoiding when I see it." He laughed as if he had a delightful secret. "Actually, I thought escaping into the tax assessor's office was funny."

As far as Olivia was concerned, *nothing* associated with C. J. Baker was funny.

He picked up her hand and drew tingly little circles on her palm. "Livy, sweetheart. We have to straighten out some things. Please have dinner with me."

Olivia jerked her hand away. "Absolutely no way. I will not—and read my lips if you're having trouble grasping this concept—I will not have an affair with a married man!"

Oops, that must've come out a little louder than she'd expected as several heads turned in their direction. Good grief! The infamous Port Serenity grapevine would spread that one within hours if not minutes.

Apparently the sheriff didn't take umbrage because he simply smiled, and what a smile he had. In his chambray shirt, tight faded jeans, well-worn boots and shiny brass star he could easily have been cast in a remake of *Butch Cassidy and the Sundance Kid*. Ooh boy! Maintaining her immunity to the guy would take a resolve of steel, but Olivia intended to do exactly that. One broken heart was plenty, thank you.

He put his arm on the back of the seat and played with her ponytail. "That's funny, I thought I said dinner." C.J. shrugged and put on a cat-in-the-creamery expression. "But an affair sounds good to me." He paused for effect. "And let me make something perfectly clear, I'm *not* married."

"Humph," she snorted as she grabbed the check and unsuccessfully attempted to push out of the booth.

GETTING OLIVIA TO forgive him would be one of C.J.'s toughest assignments, and as a former undercover narcotics cop, he was used to dealing with dangerous and difficult situations. Yep—obtaining absolution from this dark-haired beauty would require a miracle.

"Honest to God, if you'll have dinner with me, I won't kiss you or touch you. I won't even flirt with you. Cross my heart." He made an X on his chest. "But I have to explain why I didn't tell you about Selena. And we need to discuss why I didn't contact you while I was recuperating. I promise I'll be a good boy." Unfortunately, C.J. couldn't resist nuzzling her neck. She had such an appealing neck. In fact, everything about this woman was tempting.

"That does it!" Olivia swatted him. "You don't have a clue when to quit, do you?" This time she pushed him hard enough to dislodge him from the booth—not an easy feat when he was six-two and built like a pro running back.

C.J. was about to concede this round when he felt a big hand clap on his shoulder. "How's it goin'?" That voice couldn't belong to anyone but his best friend and former partner in the narcotics division, Christian Delacroix. Christian was also the man who'd risked his life to save C.J. when he was shot in an aborted drug raid.

"Not bad."

"And how's my favorite pet doc?" Christian addressed Olivia. "Neuter anyone lately?"

Olivia noticed that C.J. winced. Good. "Very funny. Everyone's a comedian. How's life as a soon-to-be daddy?"

"It's interesting," Christian said before he turned to watch Lolly, his very pregnant wife, stop at various tables to chat. Although she was on maternity leave, Lolly was still the police chief of Port Serenity.

"She says she wants to go by the office to tie up some loose ends. But if I know her, she'll be calling Sergeant Joe from the delivery room."

"She's so…so big," Olivia blurted. Lolly was her best friend and they'd been sharing thoughts, hopes and dreams since their first training bras.

Christian grinned as he sat down on the other side of the booth. "Yeah, and the word *waddle* has been erased from my vocabulary. But it'll be worth it when we get those baby girls home."

"I can't believe she's having twins," Olivia said.

"Me neither. But as long as they have all their digits and look like their mama, I'll be a happy man."

Who wouldn't be? If they looked like their mother, those kids would be drop-dead gorgeous. Where Olivia had dark brown eyes and waist-length sable hair, Lolly was a blue-eyed, natural platinum blonde.

And speaking of blondes… The blonde in question greeted half the town before she made it over to the booth. "Hey, guys." She leaned in to give Christian a kiss. "Move over. My feet are killing me." She tried to slip into the booth. "Oops. I don't think I fit." She speared Olivia with a killer look. "And if you laugh, I'll pull my gun on you."

Olivia's lips twitched.

"I'm serious. I'm licensed to use deadly force."

Olivia couldn't help it. She broke into a belly laugh. "Man alive, are you sure you're only having twins?"

Lolly joined her in the laughter. "Yes, ma'am,

just two. I know, I know. I'm the size of an elephant, but he loves me." The "he" she was talking about gently rubbed her belly. "Doc said we're going to have these babies in two weeks come hell or high water. You're planning to be there, aren't you Livy?"

"Are you kidding? I wouldn't miss this birthin' for the world. Those are my goddaughters you're talking about." Olivia took out her date book. "What's your best estimate?"

"I'm not sure. I should know more after my doctor's appointment. I'll call you as soon as I hear something."

Using Lolly as a distraction, C.J. had somehow managed to resume his spot on the bench, and slid even closer to Olivia. But before she could get rid of the pest, C.J.'s cell phone rang and then hers chirped almost simultaneously. That wasn't a good sign when the two people involved were the Aransas County sheriff and the coroner.

"What's up?" he asked and listened intently before he snapped his phone shut. "Guess you heard?" He glanced pointedly at the phone she'd just closed.

"Yeah."

C.J. brought Lolly and Christian into the conversation. "Mrs. Pomerantz found a body at the nature preserve."

"What was Mrs. Pomerantz doing at the bird sanctuary?" Lolly asked. As police chief, her jurisdiction ended at the city limits, unlike C.J.'s territory which included all 276 square miles of Aransas

County, excluding the towns of Port Serenity and Nueces Pass.

The economy of the county flourished on tourists who sipped tea at the Victorian bed-and-breakfasts, patronized the art galleries and romped in the surf. For the more nature-minded, the miles of rocky coast were dotted with sandy beaches and thickets of live oak that grew to the water's edge, providing a lush haven for exotic birds and sea creatures. Unfortunately, a secluded wilderness area could be the perfect place for murder.

Lolly's questions drew a frown from her husband. "Well, I'm just curious." She punched him on the arm. "Okay, point taken. It's out of my jurisdiction and I'm on maternity leave."

C.J. grabbed his Stetson and stood. "My deputy's on his way. I'll let you know what I find out. You want a ride?" he asked Olivia.

Not really. Just the thought of being in a car with Mr. Too-Cute-for-His-Own-Good gave her chills. But unfortunately her Corvette was in the auto shop next door—which was the reason she was sitting around Daisy's Diner in the first place. "Okay, but no funny stuff."

He graced her with that heart-stopping grin again. "I promise. Business only. Let's go." C.J. didn't give her time to change her mind before he took her hand and helped her to her feet.

"Stop it! That's exactly what I mean." Not that her protests would make any difference. Trying to squelch his gentlemanly tendencies would be like turning back the tide. Because right to his core, C.J. was a slow-walking (Lordy, that man could saunter), quick-grinning Texas charmer.

Chapter Two

"What have you been up to lately?" Olivia had to say something—the silence was driving her nuts.

C.J. glanced over and grinned. "Not much. Getting a divorce, running a campaign, buying a house—the usual stuff."

Obviously that wasn't a safe topic. But before Olivia's brain kicked in, her mouth took over. "So where *is* Selena these days?" When had she developed that masochistic streak?

C.J. didn't turn to look at her, but she could tell he was smiling. "She got a job as a physical therapist in Dallas. Same place she interned. She seems happy and I'm delighted for her. Listen—" he draped one hand negligently over the steering wheel "—I'm sorry that I never—" Before he could finish the apology, he was interrupted by the crackle of the radio.

"Sheriff, we've got two bodies out there, a man and a woman." The dispatcher was trying for a calm tone but didn't quite pull it off.

"Copy that." C.J. gunned the Explorer. "I'm fifteen minutes away and I have the coroner with me."

Olivia noted the grim expression on his face. He'd made the leap from charming rogue to consummate cop in the blink of an eye. The guy had a lot of faults, but when it came to police work he was the best. Not only was he intelligent and intuitive, he abhorred crimes involving women. All in all, he was a natural-born protector.

"Why do you think Mrs. Pomerantz was at the wildlife refuge?" he asked, even though it was obviously a rhetorical question.

Olivia was wondering the same thing. Mrs. Pomerantz was one of Port Serenity's more colorful characters. She was at least eighty and drove a mint condition '65 Impala. Everyone in town got out of the way when Mrs. Pomerantz hit the road. As for the wildlife refuge, it was wild and beautiful but it wasn't for the faint of heart. And it certainly wasn't a suitable place for a little old lady who could barely see her hand in front of her face.

"Do you think she knows about Big Bob?" Olivia asked. That was the nickname of a famous fifteen-foot gator who loved to sun himself on hot asphalt. Not to mention the cottonmouth water moccasins, javelina hogs and God only knew what else. "Last year when Lolly and I went out to look at the whooping cranes we almost ran over a ten-footer right in the middle of the road."

C.J. raised an eyebrow. "Those guys are interesting but I've been more impressed with the mosquitoes the size of '58 Buicks, with fins."

Olivia cringed at the thought of the voracious bloodsuckers. "Do you have any insect repellent?"

"Try the console."

She retrieved the lotion and liberally slathered it on. Even with repellent, she'd probably end up looking like she had chicken pox before the day was over.

C.J. whipped into the entrance of the nature preserve and roared down the gravel road to one of the bird observatories. A large bull alligator slid into the tidal marsh as they sped by. A couple of years earlier the park service had done a wildlife inventory and concluded that at least twenty thousand of the prehistoric reptiles resided in the 70,000-acre conservancy.

A pea-green Lincoln Town Car was stopped in the middle of the dirt road with its doors standing wide open. Two elderly women huddled by the front bumper, engaged in an animated discussion with one of C.J.'s young deputies.

"Curtis is getting the initiation by fire, isn't he?" he commented as he parked his Explorer next to the police cruiser.

The deputy was young, cute and obviously overwhelmed.

"Sure enough. By herself Mrs. Pomerantz is a handful, but when you add Gladys Schmidt to the equation, you quadruple the trouble," Olivia agreed.

C.J. ambled over to the cruiser. "Ladies." He tipped his hat. "I hear there's been some trouble out here." C.J. was a master at good-old-boy charm.

"Why don't you sit in my car where it's cool and tell me all about it?" It didn't take a second invitation to entice the seniors into the back seat of the Explorer. Even though it was April, the temperature was already in the 90s.

Mrs. Pomerantz was the first to pipe up. "Gladys and I decided to come out and see if any of the birds had stopped on their way up from Mexico. We went to bingo down at St. Joe's church, but Buddy Holidecker was calling and he's deafer than a post, plus he can't see squat, so we decided to beat feet."

"Yeah, we were going for ice cream but my son had given me a new pair of binoculars, so we thought we'd try them out." Gladys held up a shiny set of field glasses. "We got a little lost and when we stopped to read the sign—" she waved at an Interpretive Trail marker "—I spotted the boot."

"Yeah, and damned if it wasn't attached to a leg. Lord in heaven!" Mrs. Pomerantz exclaimed. "Not in a million years did I expect to find some dead guy in nothing but his tightie whities and a pair of ostrich-skin Tony Lamas."

C.J. noticed Olivia was having a hard time keeping her grin in check.

"And?" He encouraged the women.

"And we scurried back to the car to use the cell phone my daughter gave me." Mrs. Pomerantz paused and wiped her forehead. "Gladys's air-conditioning doesn't work too good, yours is much better. It's hotter than h-e-l-l-i-e out there." Mrs. Pomerantz was never one to mince words.

"So you didn't see anything else? No car, no people, nothing."

In unison the ladies answered in the negative.

"Tell you what. I'll have Curtis drive you home and we'll make sure you get your car back. Why don't you call someone and have them meet you? I'd rather you not go home alone."

After C.J. had the ladies situated in Curtis's cruiser he joined Olivia as she examined the man's body.

"Okay, what do we have?"

She was bagging the corpse's hands. "Look at this." Olivia held up one of the man's hands. "This guy died of carbon monoxide poisoning."

"How do you know that?"

"See how his nail beds are cherry-red?" C.J. nodded. "That didn't come from a Revlon bottle. The color is a sure-fire indication he died of carbon monoxide poisoning. Add that to the fact we don't have a gunshot wound, a knife wound or even blunt force trauma and I can do an instant diagnosis." She grinned and added a facetious note. "I'd bet my bottom dollar he didn't strip down and stroll out here to die in the wide-open spaces. That would be impossible."

"Yep, you're right. Let's check out the woman." C.J. started down the sandy path but was distracted when the ambulance arrived. "Olivia, why don't you get started?" He took a few minutes to issue orders to the attendants before he joined her.

The deceased female was lying approximately fifteen feet from the man near a large body of brackish water. She was clad in an old-fashioned slip and a pair of navy-blue pumps.

"She has the same cherry-red nails." C.J. observed as he turned the body over and held up her hand. "I sure hope we can get a match on their fingerprints because we obviously don't have any other ID."

Olivia was thankful her job was to declare the cause of death, not cut up the bodies—that fell under the purview of the medical examiner. She'd only run for the coroner's post to help pay off her vet school bills. "I'd be surprised if the autopsy revealed another cause of death. You have to have an enclosed space for fatal CO poisoning, so I suppose the questions are where did this occur and who dumped them out here for gator bait? And if it was an accident, why would someone try to dispose of the bodies."

"To state the obvious, someone wanted the gators to eat the evidence. But evidence of what?" C.J. was still contemplating the mystery when his cell phone rang.

"Hey boss, we found a half-submerged motorcycle in the saw grass."

"Don't touch it. I'll be there in a second." Whoever disposed of the bodies had probably also ditched the bike. And C.J. would definitely like to talk to that someone.

As it turned out, the new evidence included a brand-new Harley and two helmets. It didn't include clothes, identification or VIN. And that left him with nothing in his attempt to identify John and Jane Doe.

Sometimes it didn't pay to get up, and this was beginning to look like one of those days.

Olivia had joined him and was watching the deputies search for additional clues. "What do you think?"

"I don't know." C.J. verbalized his thoughts, hoping to clarify the situation. "Right now I don't even know if a crime's been committed. But I do know these folks didn't get here by themselves." Okay, that deduction didn't exactly fall in the Sherlock Holmes category, but hey! "We'll have to wait and see. If this is some kind of double suicide, it's the strangest thing I've ever seen."

"No kidding," Olivia agreed. Even for a homicide it was mysterious.

What in the world had possessed her to run for coroner? Oh yeah, the vet school bills. Maybe she should chuck the dead body gig and apply for the midnight shift at the Pac 'n' Save. At least that way she could get free Slurpees.

Chapter Three

They spent the rest of the afternoon combing the wildlife refuge and C.J. was ravenous. "How about going with me to the Sonic for supper? I guarantee I won't discuss anything more controversial than the merits of curly fries versus ranch fries."

It had been a doozy of a day. He had two corpses with some weird cause of death, and on the personal front he wasn't any closer to gaining Olivia's trust than he had been yesterday. If the grim set of the lady's chin was any indication, the chances of getting back in her good graces were slim to none, and slim had already left town.

C.J. never backed down from a challenge—the bigger, the better. His mama claimed he was flat-out mule stubborn. He preferred to think of it as determined, but whatever you wanted to call it, Dr. Olivia didn't stand a chance. C. J. Baker always got his man—or woman, as the case might be.

"Okay, but you'd better behave. I'm only agreeing because I'm starving and I haven't been to a grocery store in ages." As soon as the words left her mouth, Olivia realized she'd made a big fat mistake. This man had been responsible for one of the worst days of her life.

Every time she closed her eyes, she could vividly remember the excruciating hours she'd spent in the intensive care unit not knowing whether he was going to live or die. Then she'd relive the devastating day she discovered the man she loved, and the only man she could ever imagine spending her life with, was married to a fiery redhead who was barely old enough to buy beer.

Her family and friends tried to put a positive spin on the fiasco, but she wasn't buying any of it. Christian claimed it was a marriage in name only—just another case of C.J. adopting a stray. Supposedly, the marriage was the only way he could get Selena away from an abusive brother in Colombia.

Platonic—her rear end. He was an all-American boy with over-the-top testosterone and Selena looked like she'd stepped off the pages of *Cosmo*. What kind of idiot did everyone take her for?

Olivia tried hard to keep from thinking about Selena. But late at night she chewed on the thought like a rat on an extension cord.

True, she had avoided him like the plague since he'd quit his job as an undercover narcotics officer and returned to Port Serenity. Plus, she had ducked into the tax assessor's office when she spied him in the hall. Darn his hide—how in the world had he spotted her? Talk about embarrassing.

If he thought he could wheedle her into forgiving him, he was delusional. The guy had broken her heart and stomped on the pieces, and no one got away with messing with Olivia Alvarado. It did, however, gall her that just one of his silly grins could still send her tummy into barrel rolls. It was unfair. Not only was it unfair—it was downright dangerous to her mental health.

The moment he pulled the Explorer into the parking bay at the Sonic drive-in her appetite kicked in. Just the smell of sizzling burgers made her stomach growl. She slapped a hand over her midsection.

"This is your fault. If you hadn't been such a pest I would have finished my lunch. So, you're buying." She'd let him spring for a burger and then she'd ditch him.

"Jalapeño double cheeseburger, large fries and a tall Dr Pepper."

He grinned and those darn dimples made another appearance. "Guess there's nothing like a dead body to jump-start the old appetite, huh?"

She swatted his arm. Easy banter and teasing used to be the essence of their relationship. But those were the good old days.

"You're thinking too much." He twirled a stray strand of her hair around his finger. "Why don't you try listenin' to your heart?" Then he ran his index finger down the side of her cheek and rested it in the center of her bottom lip.

Mother Mary! When he did things like that she couldn't think, much less react. It took a few seconds for her brain to make the proper connections. "Quit it."

He chuckled and slid down his window to take their food from the carhop. "Sweetheart, you've been saved by the burger. But don't take your reprieve for granted. I promise we'll straighten this out. Don't you doubt it. Not for a minute."

Chapter Four

It had been a week since the discovery of John and Jane Doe, clad only in their skivvies and shoes. The autopsies confirmed they had died of carbon monoxide poisoning. So it looked like accidental death. The anomaly that was bothering Olivia was why someone would strip them down and put them out for alligator bait? And if by some strange turn of events it proved to be a homicide, why hadn't the victims put up a struggle? There wasn't a mark on either body.

Those niggling questions haunted Olivia's every waking hour, but it was C.J. who was really making her crazy. He was popping up everywhere. Just yesterday she'd almost bowled him over in the feminine hygiene aisle at the Super Saver. His halfhearted mumbled excuse that he was shopping was a load of bull hockey. But at least that time he'd kept his hands to himself. She wasn't quite so lucky during their encounter in the produce section of the Piggly Wiggly. That man could make fondling a peach look erotic.

Enough. Olivia refocused her attention on her

grossly overweight Chihuahua patient and his hypochondriac owner. "Mrs. Conner, if you don't get Pepe on a diet he's going to have some big medical problems. He should lose at least ten pounds." A nineteen-pound Chihuahua was not a good thing. The dog's belly was as tight as a tick.

"But he loves his treats," the owner whined. She looked like a regular patron at the Tastee Treat drive-in.

"Yes ma'am, I understand. I love chocolate, but I try to resist. Right now he's in good health, but you absolutely have to put him on a special diet."

"Doc." One of the vet techs stuck her head in the door to get Olivia's attention. "You have an emergency phone call. Should I tell him to hold?"

"Yeah. I'll be there in a sec." More than likely it was Christian announcing a trip to the maternity ward. Lolly was the size of a beached whale.

"I need to answer this phone call. Promise me, Mrs. Conner, you'll watch what Pepe eats."

"I will. I promise." Uh-huh—and Olivia believed in the tooth fairy.

"Dr. Alvarado," she answered.

Sure enough, it was Christian. "Livy, we're at the hospital. Doc says the girls will be making their grand entrance in somewhere between ten minutes and ten hours. You wouldn't believe some of the vile names Lolly's been calling me and the scary things she's threatening to do."

Olivia had to laugh. "I'll be there in a half hour. I have one more patient and then I can leave."

She quickly diagnosed a bad case of fleas, prescribed a good bug killer and was on her way to the hospital. The whole godmother thing was such a kick. The only fly in the ointment was the godfather, C. J. Baker, Christian's best friend and, duh, her current shadow.

THE WAITING ROOM of the maternity ward was decorated in generic pink plastic. And for reading material someone obviously had cleaned out the garage and contributed a stash of *Family Circle* magazines—circa 1980—to the cause. After an hour of boredom even a conversation with the future godfather seemed like a pleasant diversion.

And speaking of diversions, there he was in the flesh.

"Sorry it took me so long to get here. How are the parents-to-be?" C.J. asked.

"Lolly's okay, but Christian looks a little worse for wear. She's been giving him all kinds of hell. They just went into the delivery room." Olivia crossed her fingers. "Hopefully the babies will be here any moment."

"I love it when the big guy gets rattled."

"It is kind of funny, isn't it," Olivia agreed. "Were you out on a call?"

C.J.'s eyes crinkled in prelude to a huge grin. "Yeah, it was another Mrs. Pomerantz/Gladys Schmidt event. They ran over a guy's 'hog' in the Dollar Bonanza parking lot. I was only a block away, and it involved the ladies, so I took the call. Those women are worse than Typhoid Mary."

Once before, Mrs. Pomerantz had been the cause of a near-riot on Main Street when she was involved in an altercation with a tourist. Only Lolly's diplomacy had "convinced" the visitor to take his vacation to another beach.

"Did the guy finally understand it was his fault?"

"Yeah, sort of. It was amazing how fast he decided to settle when Mrs. Pomerantz's baby boy, Bill, arrived with his checkbook."

"Good thing he's rich as Croesus, huh?"

"Sure is," she agreed.

Their conversation was cut short by the entrance of Lolly's mother, Marcela (Mee Maw to half of Aransas County), her aunt Sissy and Lolly's children Bren and Amanda.

"Hey sweetie." Olivia hugged eleven-year-old Amanda. "Are you ready for a couple of new sisters?"

"I can't wait, Aunt Livy. This is going to be so cool," Amanda enthused. "Right, Bren?"

"Yeah, cool." Bren's endorsement was somewhat less enthusiastic.

Olivia suppressed a chuckle. To a fifteen-year-old boy, a very pregnant mother was probably embarrassing beyond belief.

"I just hope I don't have to do a bunch of babysitting." He paused and appeared to be strategizing. "Do you think I could take them to football practice?"

Olivia could see his brain working. A couple of cute babies would be an irresistible cheerleader magnet. And where a football team was holding practice, cute girls were always close by.

Her thoughts were interrupted by a nurse who informed them that Dana and Renee Delacroix had made their entrance. As soon as everyone was settled in mama's room visitors would be welcome.

Amanda bounced up and down in anticipation. "This is awesome."

Olivia wondered how long the enthusiasm would last when the cuties cried all night. "Yeah, it's nice, isn't it," she agreed.

By the time visitors were allowed into Lolly's room, the new mother looked gorgeous, the little darlings were clean and swaddled and Daddy was beaming. It was hard to imagine anyone as big and bad as Christian Delacroix cuddling a couple of babies with such a goofy grin on his face. But there he was, silly smile and all.

C.J. clapped his friend on the shoulder. "Hey, man, you have some beauties there." Actually, they kind of resembled scrunched-up little red rodents, but all babies looked alike to him. "I hope they have their mama's looks, not their dad's."

Christian punched him on the arm. "Guaranteed. I wouldn't have it any other way." He ran a finger gently down Lolly's cheek. "Are you planning to follow through with the threats you made a couple hours ago?"

She appeared to be reconsidering and then grinned. "No, I guess not. I like the family jewels just like they are."

"Thank goodness."

The scene made Olivia want to tear up, it was so

sweet. And when Christian put his arms around Bren and Amanda, his step-children, to admire the new additions to their family, she was sure she'd lose it. This was the kind of family Olivia had always wanted, too, but considering her taste in men it probably wasn't going to happen.

C.J. seemed to be watching the family interaction almost as intently as she was. Could he possibly be having some of the same feelings? Not possible. This was the same man who had failed to mention the itsy, bitsy little fact that he'd been MARRIED. Domestication was *not* in his future. But, that's what she'd thought about Christian, and look at him now.

Stop right there! Hadn't the debacle with Brian taught her anything? Wasn't the humiliation of getting left at the altar, complete with a white dress, calla lilies, and a wedding cake the size of the Empire State Building enough?

Nope. Men weren't trustworthy. And someone who failed to mention the itsy, bitsy fact that he was MARRIED sure couldn't be trusted.

Not now—not ever!

Chapter Five

Olivia's most recent encounter with C.J. had left her thoughts in a jumble. And when things got too confused, it was time to call in the expert—her mom.

Olivia parked in front of Rose McKittrick Alvarado's art gallery, the Toad and Turtle, and stared in mute fascination at the tableau that confronted her. The huge papier-mâché bowl blocking the sidewalk contained at least a half dozen people colorfully dressed as vegetables. Good grief—it was another wacky example of Mama's performance art.

Times like this Olivia wished she could twitch her nose and make it all go away, but darn it, she'd missed out on the Samantha Stevens gene.

Olivia unfolded her legs from the low-slung sports car. The gently used red Corvette had cost a fortune, and the maintenance—what can you say about sports car upkeep, but a girl had an image to maintain, and for her, the 'Vette was perfect.

She strolled up to the front of the gallery, put her hands on her hips and peered into the bowl.

"Mama, are you in there?"

Sure enough the eggplant raised its head and smiled. "Livy, sweetie. What are you doing in town this afternoon? We're practicing our still life for the festival this weekend." Rose got to her feet and leaned over to kiss Olivia's cheek.

Her mother was an eggplant. Very few people could pull off a purple spandex leotard like Rose McKittrick Alvarado. The woman was a dead ringer for Maureen O'Hara from the old John Wayne movies.

"You folks continue to contemplate life while I talk to my baby girl," Rose instructed her fellow artists and stepped out onto the sidewalk. "Come into the gallery and I'll fix us a nice glass of iced tea. It's wicked hot out here and we're still a month from summer." She fanned her face and pulled off her purple headdress. "What's up with you this afternoon?" Rose asked as she strolled to the back room that served as her office.

Olivia fingered a new display of ceramic jewelry. "Not much. I thought you might be able to go to the Blue Lagoon for lunch. I don't have any patients scheduled until two."

Rose handed Olivia the tea, cupped her chin and studied her face. Uh-oh, Olivia recognized Rose's maternal BS radar. That sucker was more accurate than the weather service.

"Is everything okay?"

"Sure. Everything's fine. I was just hungry for some of Miss Lou's chicken salad." That wasn't a total lie—she did have a hankering for a chicken salad sandwich, heavy on the mayo.

Rose paused and then nodded. "Give me fifteen minutes to get rid of this stuff." She ran a finger through the purple paint on her face. "I'd scare off all the sisters' customers if I went like this."

THE FARTHINGHAM SISTERS, Lou and Peggy, had owned the Blue Lagoon tea room since Olivia was a little girl. The tea and scone selection was limited, but the ladies made the best coconut cake and chicken salad west of the Mississippi.

It only took Rose ten minutes to ditch the purple paint and look like a million bucks. Nothing like good genes, Olivia decided as she watched her mother make her way through the crowded restaurant stopping at almost every table to chat. Not for the first time she pondered the thought that her mom would be great in politics.

"Hey there, Peggy, how's Harold's bronchitis?" Rose asked the hostess who was leading them to a premier window table.

"Not bad, not bad." Peggy laughed as she gave them the menus. "Sure has made his snorin' worse. The man sounds like a sawmill."

That tidbit fell into the "too much information" category. It was time to change the subject. "Peggy, I'd love some iced tea. I'm parched," Olivia said.

"Sure enough. How about you, hon?" the waitress asked Rose.

"Lemonade would be fabulous. And I don't need to see the menu. I'll take the tuna melt." Rose handed the menu back unopened.

"And I'd like my regular, the chicken salad sandwich with chips," Olivia said. She should probably have the arugula salad with sprouts, but a girl could only handle so many healthy things in one day and she'd already jogged three miles.

Olivia knew as well as she knew her own name that the moment Peggy left, the inquisition would begin.

Rose pulled her napkin out of its ring, snapped the fabric and dropped it in her lap. "Might as well spill it. Does this have something to do with C.J.?"

Yup—nothing got by that woman. Olivia chewed on her bottom lip. She felt like she was still in elementary school. "I guess it does. He's driving me nuts. Every time I turn around he's there, fiddling with my hair, or touching my face, or massaging my neck. I want him to leave me alone."

Rose stared at her thoughtfully. "Do you really? Or are you just afraid of getting hurt again?"

"Oh please, Mother. One time is plenty, thank you."

"Hmm." Their order came and Rose left the conversation unfinished.

Olivia took one bite and put her sandwich down. Normally in matters of the heart she'd turn to her best friend, Lolly. But Lolly had her hands full with the twins, so Mama was elected.

"Okay, I'll admit it. I still have feelings for him. I fell head over heels in love with him and he broke my heart. And worse still, he violated my trust. After my Brian experience, that's the worst kind of betrayal. Maybe if C.J. had been honest with me from the beginning, we could fix this mess. But he wasn't. If he hadn't been shot how long do you think it would have taken him to tell me about Selena?"

Rose put her hand over Olivia's. "Sweetie, sweetie, sweetie. You see the world in vivid reds and greens and blues. Other people don't have that gift. Take C.J.'s daddy, for instance. Lord, that man was a handsome devil. Anyway, he was a black-and-white kind of guy. Some of that had to have rubbed off on those boys. I think that's why C.J. and Chandler chose dangerous careers. And I think the whole black, white and gray thing is the reason C.J. held back with you. He bends the rules because he's a natural-born protector.

"I suspect he was trying to look after both you and Selena. He was waiting for the perfect time to tell you; unfortunately, everything got mucked up before the perfect time arrived." Rose took a bite of her tuna melt before she continued. "Corrine told me he was all torn up about what happened between the two of you."

Olivia couldn't resist an eloquent snort. "Mrs. Baker's a nice lady, but she doesn't know what a sleazoid her son is."

"Really?"

"Yeah, really." Olivia paused. "Well, no, he's not. Not really."

Rose continued to eat. "Did you know that C.J.'s divorce is final and Selena has a job in Dallas?"

"Mother!"

"I think you should give your heart another chance. But, I'll change the subject." Rose discontinued her motherly advice. "You remember my friend Connie Lee, don't you?" Rose continued without waiting for an answer. "She was the tomato in our still life. Anyway, she told me the most fascinating thing."

Olivia mentally winced. When Mama started the conversation with words like fascinating it was time to become scarce.

"Have you heard about the Bayou Church of the Saved Sinners?" Rose asked.

Everyone in town had heard about the congregation that had taken up residence in an abandoned chicken processing plant.

"I'd like for you to go with me to one of their services."

Mother Mary! Rumor had it that the Bayou Church services were a unique combo of West Indian voodoo, biker rally and country/western revival.

"I think it would be a great place to get some new song material." Rose was an aspiring country/western songwriter. "Plus, I think it would be fun. We can make it a girls' adventure."

"I suppose that depends on your idea of fun," Olivia responded.

"Connie Lee said the place still smells like wet chicken feathers."

"You're definitely on your own."

Rose finished her lunch. "The preacher's name is Wilbur Hardaway and his wife is Florene." She paused for dramatic emphasis. "Connie says Florene has these honkin' big hooters that aren't quite perky anymore. And on one of them she has this tattoo that says Hallelujah in script over the picture of a rose. Except the script is running down into her cleavage so all you can see is Hell." Rose started laughing and couldn't stop. "The tattoo artist apparently misspelled Hallelujah. Connie claims the rose looks like a deflated balloon." Rose had another attack of the giggles. "And Brother Wilbur is a dead ringer for the fat Elvis."

Despite herself, Olivia began to laugh, too. Only Mama could entice her to attend the Bayou Church of the Saved Sinners. "Okay, I give. You couldn't rope Daddy into this one, huh?"

"Are you kidding? He said if Aunt Emelda found out I went to that place she'd put *el mal ojo* on me. Good Lord, the evil eye can ruin your whole week."

"Ain't that the truth."

When Mama failed to maintain eye contact Olivia was sure the next shoe was about to drop.

"They're having their Hog Heaven rally next Sunday. I thought that would be interesting."

"Hog Heaven?"

"Yeah, it's a blessing of the bikes." Rose chuckled. "They probably need some heavenly intervention to keep from getting killed. Think about it, a Harley rally at a church. Can't you just hear the song now—I wiped off my tattoo on I-35." Rose hummed a few bars of her newest creation.

Holy catfish! That was one scary gene pool.

C.J. WAS ON HIS WAY back to the office after a *very* long day. His office had coordinated the trailer park drug bust of a married couple who'd cooked meth-amphetamines in their kitchen, right in front of their kids. Some people had their heads so far up their butts they'd never see daylight.

He was busy contemplating felonious characters when he spied Livy's sports car in front of the Blue Lagoon. That bright red, dual-carburetor speed machine was hard to miss in a typical Port Serenity sea of pickups and Suburbans, but it perfectly matched Dr. Alvarado's personality—fiery and im-pressive.

C.J. pulled his Explorer over to the curb. The Blue Lagoon was way too girly for his taste but he'd chow down on endive and caviar if it gave him an opportu-nity to talk to Livy. He was about to step out of the SUV when she pranced onto the street. There wasn't any other way to describe how she walked. With her showgirl legs, silky sable ponytail and exotic eyes she could be the subject of any man's red-hot Latin fantasy.

And if the old saying about checking out the mom for a preview of the future was true, Olivia was going to be stunning till the day she died. Because Rose Al-varado, with her flaming red hair, still turned heads. She was a true daughter of the Emerald Isle.

The ladies hopped into the Corvette and Olivia peeled out almost before Rose had her door closed. It was a typical Livy exit—the cloud of burning rub-ber and a rooster tail of sprayed gravel.

Life with that woman would never be boring.

Chapter Six

Mama had great insight but there were some things a girl didn't discuss with her mother. So two days later Olivia found herself on Lolly's porch listening to a soft lullaby coming from inside the house. Things must be good on the home front. She didn't hear any crying babies or loud teenage music, just a soft lilting song. Olivia simultaneously tapped on the door frame and opened the screen.

"It's me."

"Back in the den," Lolly responded. "We're having a tea party." She had one child clasped to her breast while she pushed a bassinet with her foot. "It's called multitasking. And I used to think running a police department was demanding."

Olivia took over the job of rocking the bassinet, which held a sleeping baby. "Where is everyone?"

"Amanda's at Leslie's house." Lolly popped the food supply out of Dana's greedy mouth. "I think the new is about to wear off these two. Bren's at baseball practice and Christian had to run in to Corpus for a meeting with his captain."

"How does Christian like manning a desk?" Olivia asked. Christian had been an undercover narcotics cop when he met his future wife, but love, children and a white picket fence had enticed him into the relatively safe world of law enforcement management. Now he was the head of the Corpus Christi office of the Department of Public Safety Narcotics Division.

Lolly hoisted the baby to her shoulder and was rewarded with a big burp. "Sometimes I think he misses the adrenaline rush, but this job gives him the chance to handle the big picture." She gave Dana a few love pats. "Let me see if I can get this one down and we'll have something cold to drink."

"Which twin is that?" Olivia asked.

Lolly pondered the question. "I'm not really sure. I'm fairly positive this cutie is Dana, but sometimes I get confused." She shrugged. "I'm thinking about marking the bottoms of their feet with an indelible marker." She gently placed the sleeping baby in the second bassinet. "Let's go while we can."

They tiptoed into the kitchen, where Lolly fell into a chair. "Lord, Livy, I'm exhausted. I don't remember babies being this much work. Of course, I only had one at a time."

Olivia fixed two glasses of tea. This obviously wasn't a good moment to dump on her friend, who had more than enough to deal with. "So you're not ready to go to Cotton-Eyed Joe's and kick up your heels, huh?"

Lolly rubbed her back. "Are you kidding? My current fantasy is to go to a motel by myself, turn the air conditioner down till I have frost on my nose and sleep for a week. So let me live vicariously and tell me what's happening out in your world."

"Not much. We still haven't figured out how the bodies got to the wildlife refuge. C.J. has run their descriptions and fingerprints through every database available, but he can't identify them. The case has everyone baffled. But I suppose you've been keeping track of everything associated with murder and mayhem in and around Port Serenity, haven't you?"

Lolly gave her a guilty grin. "Yep. It drives Christian wild, but I feel compelled to check in with Sgt. Joe every day. It's my lifeline to a world of adult conversation. And speaking of C.J...."

Olivia raised her hand. "I don't remember speaking of that man." Although a down and dirty discussion of life, love and Sheriff C. J. Baker held enormous appeal. And even though Lolly was terrific at weeding through the junk and picking out the important things, Olivia resisted the lure—momentarily.

"But if you insist. Do you know what that cretin did last week?" Olivia leaned forward as if she was about to whisper a secret. "He followed me to the Piggly Wiggly and cornered me in the dairy section. Then he kissed me silly right in front of the yogurt shelf. Half the town was in the grocery store for double-coupon day. And when I smacked him, he put on that cocky grin of his and sauntered off like he owned the world. He's going to be the death of me."

Lolly stared at her friend for a few seconds and then burst into gales of laughter. She had to wipe her eyes with the bottom of her T-shirt, she was laughing so hard.

Olivia couldn't believe it. She had bared her soul and Lolly had the audacity to think the situation was funny. Olivia's drop-dead glare stopped the belly laughs for a few moments, but then they started again.

"I'm so glad I'm entertaining." Sarcasm dripped off every word. "Do you really think after that fiasco ten years ago with Brian, and my more recent encounter with C.J.'s duplicity, I could ever get snookered by a man again?"

Lolly nodded seriously. "You have a point there. I've still got that awful lavender bridesmaid dress. Amanda plays dress-up in it."

Olivia wasn't about to admit she had her wedding dress stuffed in the back of her closet. That was her secret and her reminder to be *very* careful with her heart.

"But," Lolly continued, "C.J. is not Brian and the whole Selena debacle—" she waved a hand in the air "—was just a massive screw-up. Honey, believe me, he's not going to hurt you again."

"Ha!"

Lolly hugged her best friend. "Boy, are you articulate. I love you to death but you're the biggest dingbat on the Gulf Coast. Admit it—the man will eventually wear you down and I'm gonna love watching you take the plunge."

"He absolutely is not going to get to me."

"Oh, yeah, he is."

Olivia could feel her stubborn coming on—damn it, she hated that particular character flaw. "Want to bet?"

When Lolly got that sly look on her face Olivia knew she was in trouble.

"I'll make it easy on you." Lolly put on the grin Livy hated. "If within a year you two aren't engaged, I'll take you to Mexico for a week and pay for everything. If at the end of that time you have a rock on your finger, we'll still go to Mexico, but you're paying. Either way, I get a week in the sun." Lolly laughed. "Now I just have to convince my big lug of a husband that he'll want to babysit for a week."

"Okay, you're on but it's a sucker bet. And read my lips here. C. J. Baker and I do *not* have a future. So if you still want to wager, it's your pocketbook." Olivia stuck out her hand to shake on the deal. This one was a no-brainer. An engagement ring was not on the horizon. Never, never, ever.

THE NEXT DAY Olivia was sitting at her desk thinking about sunny beaches and drinks with paper umbrellas when her official coroner phone rang. Darn it.

"Dr. Alvarado," she answered.

Double darn! It was the dispatcher from the sheriff's office. "Hey, doc, Sheriff Baker asked me to call you. A bunch of kids found some bones out near the old refinery and he'd like you to come. They're in a field near the gravel pit. You can't miss 'em."

"Okay." She was making a mental inventory of

her morning patients. "Tell him I'll be there in about twenty minutes."

Olivia buzzed the receptionist. "I have a coroner emergency. Would you please tell Dr. Bob what's happening and ask him to take the rest of my patients." After she'd made the necessary arrangements, Olivia grabbed her bag and ditched her strappy sandals—fashionable footwear and the soft muck of a south Texas cotton field didn't mix.

The police cruisers' emergency lights created an almost carnival atmosphere, but any situation involving a possible crime was far from festive. When Olivia drove her car onto the grassy shoulder she noticed a group of men congregated near the pumping units. The machinery that pulled the oil from the earth had always reminded her of huge crickets. Up and down, up and down—the motion was mesmerizing.

C.J. was talking to one of his deputies when Olivia walked up, so she waited until he finished. "What's happening?"

"The kids were playing paintball and found bones in the creek bed. I suspect the heavy rains we had last winter washed them down here and it just took a while for someone to find them."

Olivia glanced at two boys sitting on the ground— the color leached completely from their faces. Then she noticed the bright red and green splotches on the scrub oak. "Paintball?"

"Yeah, I didn't know this was the new battleground, but apparently it's quite popular." C.J. waved a hand to indicate the trees covered in paint. "Come take a look and tell me what you think."

His professionalism always astonished Olivia. In situations like this, he was all business. No cocky grin, no dimples, no flirting. It was like a switch he could turn on and off at will.

They picked their way through the sandy terrain to the edge of the creek where, sure enough, there were some bones. The question was, were they human? Olivia snapped on her gloves and knelt to get a better look.

She conducted as thorough an examination as she could in the field. "In my professional opinion these came from a deer. But since I don't have a skull, I can't be one hundred percent positive. About ninety-nine percent, though." She stood and pulled off her latex gloves. "I'd suggest you send them to the medical examiner in Corpus for confirmation."

"Sounds like a plan to me," C.J. agreed. Although he was wearing aviator sunglasses, he shaded his eyes and peered at the road. "The ambulance is here." He turned back to Olivia. "You're pretty sure it's a deer?"

"Yeah."

C.J. nodded and called over his two detectives. Deputies were roping off the area with yellow crime-scene tape. "Go ahead and scour the place, although I don't think we have a crime scene. Get the deputies to help you and let me know right away if you find anything significant." The men nodded and started their search.

The bones were bagged and put on the gurney awaiting transportation while the investigation continued.

"We've done everything we can out here," C.J. said. "We dodged a bullet, no pun intended, on this one." That hadn't been the case the previous summer, when dead drug dealers washed up on the beach in Port Serenity.

"Why don't you follow me to the Tastee Treat? I missed lunch and I'm starving. We can talk about the case," C.J. suggested.

Olivia contemplated his invitation for a moment. It wasn't fair to lead him on—but it was just a quick lunch. "Oh, all right. But I have to be back at the clinic by two."

"I'll eat fast, I promise." He grinned as he followed her across the field. That was some view—and it wasn't the landscape he was admiring.

THE DOWNSIDE OF the Tastee Treat was that it was the local high school hangout. The upside was they made the best burgers in the county.

"Double cheeseburger, large onion rings, and a strawberry shake." C.J. placed his order with the blond ponytailed cutie behind the counter.

When he flashed her one of his dimpled grins, the kid almost swooned. For heaven's sake! Sure, the guy looked like he'd stepped right out of a sexy Western. But was that any reason for every female in town to get all google-eyed?

The teenager was still checking out C.J. when

Olivia walked up to the counter. She cleared her throat to get the kid's attention.

"Grilled cheese sandwich and a Diet Coke."

Her order elicited a smile from Mr. Hot and Sexy.

"What happened to the woman who ordered the jalapeño double cheeseburger at the Sonic?"

"Stuff it, Baker." Olivia marched to an empty booth at the back of the restaurant and sat down.

C.J. followed her, but instead of sitting across the table, he sank down next to her.

What was it with booths and this guy? Everyone knew you didn't leave one side of the booth empty.

Then he ran his fingers through her ponytail. Why was he stroking her hair? She pushed his hand away, eliciting a chuckle.

"I've wanted to do this all day." He began with her neck and proceeded to place a string of soft, wet kisses between her nape and her jaw.

"Hmm." Olivia closed her eyes and savored every one of those tingling kisses—until her brain finally engaged.

"Stop that. We're in public."

"That's not what you were thinking a minute ago."

"What, now you're a mind reader?" If all else failed, she could always count on sarcasm. It was one of her more reliable talents.

"Nope. Only with you. Your heart's telling you one thing. Your brain is on another frequency." He took one more nibble of her neck. "Your heart is gonna win, you know."

"Not in this lifetime!" At least she hoped she

could keep her resolve in place and her heart defended.

C.J.'s dimples made another appearance. "We'll see, sweetheart. We'll see."

Chapter Seven

The things Olivia did for her mother. If she hadn't been so preoccupied with Mr. Dimples she would've been able to come up with some logical excuse to skip the Bayou Church shindig. But when Mama called, Olivia was still in a tizzy about C.J.'s "we'll see."

Madre de Dios! What *did* you wear to a Harley hoedown? Olivia frowned as she pulled out a mini-skirt, tossed it on the bed, and rummaged through the bottom of the closet for some appropriate shoes. For a fraction of a second she considered phoning Lolly to see if she had a blouse with a Peter Pan collar, but then she got a grip, whacked herself upside the head and reached back in the closet to retrieve a T-shirt.

The squeak of the screen door announced Rose's arrival. "Livy, honey. Are you ready?"

"Gimme a sec. There's some tea in the fridge."

Olivia pulled her waist-length hair up into a pony-tail, dabbed on some mascara and called it good. This little adventure wasn't her idea, so why did she care what she looked like? She grabbed her purse and went to the kitchen.

"Mama, that's a great outfit." Rose had somehow walked the fine line between secular and sacred in pairing tight black leather pants with a white silk blouse. "But it's almost ninety degrees outside and you're gonna bake in all that leather."

Rose nodded in agreement. "I thought about that, but I couldn't resist."

"Then let's do it." Olivia hooked arms with her mother. Even though the scenario was strange beyond belief she was determined to have a good time.

Her resolve lasted until she pulled into the temporary parking lot and checked out the sea of motorcycles. "Oh my God, look at that!" Olivia exclaimed. There were motorcycles of every size, shape and description. Ditto for the riders. They spanned the spectrum—male, female, fat, skinny, young, scruffy, yuppie, all the way to downright scary. About the only thing they had in common was leather. It was a sea of cowhide.

"Oh dear," Rose breathed. "Maybe this wasn't such a good idea."

Amen! But Olivia was determined to make the best of a bad situation. She threw back her shoulders and started across the field to the front of the church. "We've come this far, we might as well stick it out. And swear to goodness, I'll deck the first jerk who tries to put a paw on me."

"Oh, dear. I guess we'll just have to make sure that doesn't happen, won't we?" Rose said. "Look." She pointed in the direction of a large white tent. "There are some local folks and they're handing something out. Let's see what's happening."

"Okay," Olivia agreed. That, in fact, sounded like a great idea. It also sounded like shade and something cold to drink. Her darned sandals were not made for walking across a plowed field.

By the time they made it to the tent, perspiration was running between her breasts. So much for glowing like a good Southern girl—she was sweating like a pig. Her mother, however, appeared immune to the heat and humidity.

"How do you do that?"

"Do what?" Rose asked.

"Look like you just got out of the shower. Darn it, I feel like I just ran a marathon." Olivia pulled out the hem of her T-shirt and waved it to get a breeze on her overheated skin.

Two strong arms came around her waist, pinning her arms to her side. "Please don't do that." It was the warm velvet drawl she knew so well. "Watching you makes me hot." He nuzzled the side of her neck.

"C.J.," she squeaked, then regained her composure. He was the last person she expected to see at Hog Heaven. But of course he'd be here; he was the county sheriff. And although bike riding was "in" with the affluent yuppie crowd, there was still a dangerous element more traditionally associated with the sport.

C.J. twirled Olivia in his arms. "Yep, that's a cute outfit. Don't you think so, Mom?" He addressed his comment to his mother who was standing next to him.

Corrine Baker was tall, blond, statuesque…and wearing black leather chaps, a halter top and an American flag do-rag on her head. Somehow, some way, the woman who had run the library system for the past twenty-five years had morphed into a biker babe.

Good heavens, were all the baby boomers flippin' out?

"Lordy, Corrine, I haven't seen you in a month of Sundays." Rose hugged her friend. "You're looking mighty good."

Corrine put a hand on her hip to show off her chaps. "Thanks. We're not too bad for a couple of old chicks, huh? Have you met my new stockbroker, Dan Matthews?" She pulled a tall, handsome man into the conversation. "Dan got me interested in bikes."

Okay, that explained the chaps and the do-rag.

"I don't have my own wheels yet, but Dan said he'd help me find the perfect bike."

It was obvious this guy was more than just a stockbroker to Corrine. Olivia glanced at C.J. just in time to catch a brief grimace. Attending a function with your mom's date had to be tough.

"Come with us to buy a T-shirt," Corrine said to Rose. "I want the one with the cross and the motorcycle. I'm afraid they'll run out." She pulled her friend to the other side of the tent, leaving C.J. and Olivia alone.

"I didn't expect to see you here." C.J. cupped her

elbow and led her to some metal folding chairs in an out-of-the-way corner.

"Mama wanted to come and Daddy wouldn't be caught dead at something like this, so I was elected."

"Yep, my mom has a great way with a guilt trip, too. Claimed I needed to trot along as her bodyguard. She failed to tell me she was also bringing Dan the Man." C.J. shrugged. "This boyfriend thing is hard for me."

"I can imagine."

He motioned toward Corrine, Rose and Dan who were laughing with a couple of middle-aged men. "The guy on the right is a banker and the one on the left is a podiatrist. Can't tell a book by its cover, huh?"

It didn't escape Olivia's attention that while they were having this conversation C.J. was holding her hand, idly rubbing circles on her palm. She wondered whether he even realized what he was doing, or if all the touches and caresses were simply an ingrained part of his personality. For C.J., charm was as natural as breathing. Her first assumption was that he saw her as a challenge, but could all the attention be indicative of something more important? Now that was a thought to ponder.

Olivia pulled her hand away. She hated it when one of those ideas popped up like a lightbulb in a cartoon strip.

"Jeez, would you look at those two." He pointed at a man and woman who had joined Rose and Corrine.

Olivia stifled a giggle. "You don't suppose that's Brother Hardaway and Florene, do you?"

C.J. put on a wry grin. "I'd bet my bottom dollar

on it. I don't know anyone else in this town who would actually wear an Elvis suit when it wasn't Halloween."

The man in question was middle-aged and sported a Brylcreem pompadour. He was encased top to toe in a white leather jumpsuit that was unzipped almost to his navel. An ornate silver cross was nestled in a clump of black chest hair.

Yeew!

And Florene—what could you say about Florene? Stiletto heels, big, big hair, and enough makeup to make Max Factor jealous. And sure enough, the misspelled "Hellelujah" script looked more like "Hell" with the "elujah" missing in action.

"Let's go meet 'em. There's something out of whack about those two," C.J. muttered.

"No kidding." Olivia agreed.

C.J. smiled as he pulled her out of the chair. "I'm talking about more than the obvious."

Olivia couldn't imagine what that might be. In this town, everyone over the age of forty was certifiably insane.

Chapter Eight

Florene Hardaway was carrying on an animated conversation, fluttering her hands in the air like a demented bird. Unfortunately, Corrine and Rose seemed to be entranced and that could only spell trouble with a capital *T*.

"It's just so much fun. And you guys know so many people." Florene continued her monologue.

Uh-oh. The ditzy duo didn't need any help dreaming up wacky schemes.

"I'll tell ya for sure, a Sara Belle party is about the most fun a girl can have with her clothes on," Florene proclaimed.

Talk about a strange comment from a preacher's wife.

"So how 'bout it? Can I count on one of you to have a party? There's a great hostess gift."

C.J. looked about as clueless as a guy at a bridal shower.

Olivia whispered, "I'll tell you later."

As Florene proceeded with her sales pitch, Rose glanced at Corrine and shrugged.

"Raul would have a coronary if I had a Sara Belle party at our house," Rose said.

"And my place is too small. I can barely get my entire family in there for Thanksgiving."

In unison, the two women turned to Olivia.

She backed away and raised her hands. "Absolutely not."

"Livy, sweetie. You have such a nice big house and Corrine and I will take care of everything. We'll clean and bring the refreshments." Rose squeezed her daughter's arm. "It'll be so much fun. You can invite your friends and we'll invite ours. We'll make it a mother-daughter event." Corrine nodded in agreement.

Olivia turned to C.J. for moral support, but the chicken-hearted man simply shrugged. Smart guy. Getting in the middle of a girly thing was a no-win situation.

She should probably just throw in the towel because in the long run she wouldn't win. Besides, she'd get a scrubbed bathroom out of the deal and Olivia was never one to turn up her nose at a sparkling toilet.

"Okay, I'll do it. But I'll hold you to the house-cleaning."

C.J. pulled her away while the two mothers discussed the logistics of the event. "Okay, what's a Sara Belle party?" he asked.

Olivia couldn't suppress her giggle. "Think of a cross between Mary Kay and Frederick's of Hollywood—sexy lingerie, stiletto heels, big hair, mongo mascara, the whole enchilada—all modeled in the comfort of your own family room. Trust me." She held up her hand as if she was swearing on a Bible. "I've never been to one of those things, but I've got friends who have." Olivia confided, "They said you wouldn't believe the lacy garter belts."

C.J. turned a bright pink. Now *that* was something.

He quickly recovered from his initial reaction and plastered on a smirk that registered somewhere between lewd and ludicrous. "Am I invited?"

"No way, Jose. And don't even *consider* crashing."

Before he could make a token protest, the ceremony began. Even considering the unique format, C.J. was struck by Brother Hardaway's unorthodox version of religion. The program started out like a modified St. Francis of Assisi blessing of the pets and then quickly changed into a Texas A&M pep rally combined with an evangelical tent revival.

C.J.'s cop antenna went on high alert. There was something not quite right about the Reverend and Mrs. Hardaway. And when something didn't pass the smell test, it made C.J. very uncomfortable, indeed.

Chapter Nine

"I can't believe I'm doing this." Olivia and Lolly were surveying the chaos that reigned in Olivia's living room. Lingerie littered every available surface and a chorus of female voices ebbed and flowed like the tide.

"This is worse than the twins at feeding time," Lolly commented before she bit into another stuffed mushroom. "But the refreshments are good." She took a sip of her mimosa. "It's been *ages* since I had anything alcoholic. One little mimosa is enough to relax me."

As far as Olivia was concerned this debacle was anything but relaxing. She glanced into the dining room, where Florene was holding court over the makeover area. Her first volunteer "victim" had been Marcela, Lolly's mom. The woman was a natural beauty with silver hair and bright blue eyes. But right this minute she could pass for a cousin of Bozo the Clown.

Lolly took another sip of her drink. "Do you think Florene uses a trowel to slather that stuff on?"

"I don't know, but I'm not going to be one of her guinea pigs," Olivia stated with authority. She'd take a stand and mean it, by gosh!

A crescendo of feminine giggles came from the bedroom where some women were trying on lingerie. "I hate to even ask, but what do you suppose they're doing back there?" Olivia honestly didn't think she wanted to know.

"Talkin' sex. You can't get a roomful of women together without the topic turning to the subject of s-e-x. So if you throw in a couple of boas and lacy teddies what do you expect?"

"Livy sweetie, we need you in here." Uh-oh, that sounded like a maternal summons.

Sure enough, Rose was standing in the door, a vision in an ivory lace nightgown and robe. She put one hand on her hip. "You think your daddy will like this?"

Lord in heaven! She would *not* have this conversation with her mother.

"We have something in here that will look absolutely stunning on you," Rose announced as several of the party-goers joined her. "And believe me, not one of us could pull this off." She held up a scrap of red lace. "Come on, be a sport."

"Might as well face the music. You don't have a chance against them." Lolly waved a hand in the direction of the women.

These ladies were pillars of the community, and right now they were twittering like a bunch of junior high girls. One of the culprits was a county commissioner and another ran a multi-million-dollar corporation.

Despite Olivia's grumbling, the fashion show went on, and on, and on. Marcela sashayed around in a silk lounging outfit, Rose preened in virginal white lace, Lolly fed her face and giggled, and Olivia hid in the bedroom dreading the moment she had to bare this thing, this tiny, tiny thing.

"Livy, get your rear end out there," Lolly demanded.

With a friend like that, who needed an enemy?

"Now! We want to see the red one." The red one was a minuscule lace teddy with a cover-up. Cover-up, her bare butt. Olivia had never been shy and her self-esteem meter was in good working order, but this was way over the top.

"Now *that's* an outfit!" Lolly glared at the cookie she was holding. "I'd have to lose a ton of baby fat to get into that. They're waiting for you."

"Okay, okay. I'm going." Olivia threw back her shoulders, plastered on her best beauty-pageant smile and strolled out to catcalls and clapping. But before she could do her first pirouette, Florene handed her a horrendously ugly pink papier-mâché piggy bank.

"That's the hostess gift. Take good care of it. It'll bring you luck." Florene winked and her false eyelashes fluttered like giant caterpillars. "A big hand for our hostess," she boomed.

The ladies showed their appreciation with whistles, claps and rude comments. Getting into the spirit of the evening, Olivia did a couple of runway turns but stopped short when someone started pounding furiously on the door.

"Good lord, what now?" she asked in general, not expecting an answer. It was probably her crabby neighbor. The one who'd had his humor bone excised at birth and wanted everyone else in the neighborhood to be as miserable as he was. Well, this time she'd give him something to think about.

Olivia marched to the door and flung it open. "Listen here—" Uh-oh. It was Sheriff C. J. Baker. His slow, lazy perusal started at her red satin mules and made a long trip upward. The look he gave her could have fried circuits all the way to Houston.

C.J. cleared his throat. "Livy, I need to come in."

Olivia paused, but then stepped aside. It was hard to deny him anything when he put on his serious professional face.

He took off his ball cap and faced a room full of women in various stages of dress and undress. "Ladies, we've had a report of a Peeping Tom. He was seen hanging around Livy's window. But don't panic. I have several deputies outside and apparently he's gone. However, I think we need to break up the party."

Olivia had never seen a bunch of females scatter so quickly. In a matter of minutes, they were history. Even Florene had abandoned her merchandise with a promise to come by tomorrow to help clean up.

"Mama, why don't you and Mrs. Baker go on home? I'll be fine with C.J. and Lolly." Olivia tightened the belt of her old terry-cloth robe.

Rose kissed her daughter's cheek. "Are you sure?" I'll pop over early in the morning and help you with the mess." She turned to C.J. "Are you sure everything's safe?"

"Yes, ma'am. It's perfectly fine." C.J. and his deputies had scoured the area and any bad guys were long gone.

Olivia lived in a well-kept '70s ranch in one of the nicest areas of Aransas County. The calls the sheriff's office usually got from these folks were barking dog complaints, so a Peeping Tom was highly unusual.

"Okay. I'm going home. Let me know if you need me," Rose instructed Olivia.

Lolly waited until the two older ladies were out the door before she started the inquisition. "What's the deal?"

C.J. grabbed a couple of stuffed mushrooms. "I don't know. Bill Throckmorton from next door was walking his dog and spotted a guy lurking out front. When he saw Bill he took off like a scalded dog."

Lolly nodded and returned her service revolver to her purse. "I didn't know we were having a problem with burglars."

"I didn't either," C.J. admitted. This didn't feel like a burglar or even a Peeping Tom, but considering the sight of Olivia in that red teddy, anything was possible.

Chapter Ten

Transitioning from the narcotics division to the sheriff's office had taken a bit of adjustment. The workload was sometimes frenetic but most of the time it was slow and easy. Today fell into the coma-inducing category. And since C.J. was busy indulging in a red-hot fantasy about a certain dark-haired beauty in a red teddy, he appreciated a yawner.

He'd just settled in with a second cup of coffee and a boring report when the phone rang. It was the desk sergeant, a remnant of the previous sheriff's regime, and to put a positive spin on the situation, he was a total jerk.

"Boss, there's some woman here to see you. She won't take no for an answer and won't give me her name." The man paused and C.J. could imagine him smirking. "But she's some looker."

He really had to do something about the guy. If nothing else, he had to get him away from the public.

"That's enough of that. I'll be right out. Ask her to have a seat," he instructed. "And be nice about it."

Before he even made it to the lobby he heard a very feminine, and familiar, voice blessing out the erstwhile desk sergeant. Leave it to Selena. The poor guy didn't realize that going head-to-head with her was like attending a gunfight armed with a knife. As tempted as C.J. was to let her shred the jerk, he took pity.

He threw open the door and held out his arms. "Selena, sweetie, what are you doing here?"

Before he knew it he was bowled over by a gorgeous redhead. "Oh, C.J!"

He pushed her back a fraction of an inch to look into her face. Tears had pooled in her emerald eyes and considering this was Selena, that wasn't a good sign. One crystalline drop would undoubtedly unleash a fountain of moisture.

"Let's go back to my office and I'll get you something cold to drink. Then you can tell me what's wrong." He slid his arm around her shoulders and ushered her down the corridor.

"Hold all my calls, I don't care who it is," he yelled at the desk sergeant. "Take a message and tell them I'll call 'em back."

"Yes sir, boss."

Once he had Selena safely in his office, a cold can of Coke in her possession and the hysteria at bay, he figured it was safe to do a little questioning.

He sat next to her on the old leather couch, holding her hand. "Okay honey, what's the problem?" Later, he'd try to figure out why she was in Port Serenity instead of Dallas.

She sniffled quietly. "I think someone is stalking me." The sniffle became more pronounced. "Last night I went to the mall, you know the one with the Lillie Rubin store. They had this great off-the-shoulder top. It's gorgeous—turquoise with all these rhinestones."

C.J. cupped her chin. "Focus."

"Okay. Well, anyway, there's this ice-skating rink in the center of the mall and I was watching the kids when I felt the hair stand up on the back of my neck. You know, it was like someone was staring." She paused and took a sip of her drink. "So I glanced across the rink and there's this guy watching me."

"That's not unusual. You're a beautiful woman."

"Yeah, well, that wasn't the first time I saw him. I noticed him outside my office and then I accidentally ran into his cart in the grocery store."

It did sound suspicious, but C.J. couldn't discount the idea that the guy was merely smitten. Selena was a captivating woman. With her fiery red hair and voluptuous body she could easily pass for a 1950s bombshell.

"So what else happened? I'm sure you wouldn't have driven six hours just to tell me some guy's following you around because he's too chicken to ask you out."

Selena added a hiccup to the sniffles. "When I got home I could tell someone had been in my apartment. Things were out of place. It looked like someone had pawed through my mail and there was a strange smell. Sort of like the market in Matamoros. Plus, for at least two weeks, I've had this weird feeling someone was watching me. And—" she paused for emphasis "—the guy looked very familiar."

"Familiar how?"

"I'm not sure. Like someone I used to know. But that's not possible. How could someone from Colombia find me in Dallas?"

That was something C.J. would like to figure out. When he'd met Selena, she was a skinny big-eyed teenager trying to blend into the woodwork so she wouldn't be noticed by her drug-lord brother's friends—a role that C.J. had assumed in his life as an undercover narcotics cop.

The first night he saw her she was cowering in a corner, fending off the unwanted advance of some gringo blubber butt. It was only a matter of time before Enrique Bolivar, Selena's brother and a true spawn of the devil, realized she wasn't a little girl anymore and decided to sell her off to the highest bidder. The scumbag had, after all, been grooming her in etiquette and English since she was a toddler—waiting for the right buyer.

The whole idea was so disgusting, C.J. had decided he had to save her. So he slipped her out of the compound and the country, and with the help of some high-placed friends he'd managed to get her into the U.S. with a new, and untraceable, identity. However, in order for the plan to work, C.J. had had to agree to a platonic marriage. With one stroke of a pen he'd acquired the little sister he'd always wanted.

C.J. pulled her into his arms. "Oh, honey, don't worry. We'll sort this out." He could only hope he was telling the truth, and furthermore, he prayed the truth wasn't what he feared.

"Tell you what." He grabbed a Kleenex off the desk and dabbed at her tears. "I'll take you to lunch. I'll bet they have some of that strawberry pie you love." He tweaked her nose. "How does that sound?"

C.J. was rewarded with a faint giggle. "Then I'll take you to Mom's house."

"Can't I stay with you?"

"Oh, honey, if you crash at my place, Olivia will have a fit. And then I can kiss my chances with her goodbye."

Selena was fully aware of the Olivia situation. During C.J.'s convalescence from a bullet wound they'd had numerous conversations about life, love and the future.

"Okay, let's go eat. I'm probably blowing this out of proportion."

C.J. hoped so. Enrique Bolivar was one nasty dude and he wouldn't put anything past him. If the guy stalking Selena was one of Enrique's goons, how had they managed to find her?

Chapter Eleven

"Hey, buddy, what's up?" Christian Delacroix inquired as he slapped his friend on the back and fell into the booth. On the jukebox George Strait was crooning about lost love. The click of billiard balls and the rumble of loud conversation provided the background noise at the Lone Star Tavern, where C.J. and Christian had a standing beer date every Thursday afternoon. But this was a Tuesday, and Christian had dropped everything when his friend called.

C.J. rubbed the bridge of his nose. If things were going down as he suspected, he'd have to bring in the big guns. And Christian Delacroix was one of the biggest guns around.

"Selena's in town."

"Oh?" Christian had had the unfortunate experience of introducing Selena to Olivia back during C.J.'s infamous stay in the intensive care unit.

"Yeah. She left Dallas because she's pretty sure someone's following her."

Christian leaned forward. "Really?" He cut his

answer short when the waitress appeared to take his order. "Shiner Bock on tap, please."

When she left, he continued. "Do you think it's some idiot who saw her at the grocery store and doesn't have the *cojones* to ask her out?"

"When you're as gorgeous as Selena, that's always a possibility, but I think something else is going on. She says the guy seems familiar, like maybe someone she saw in Colombia."

"Crap!" Christian exclaimed.

"My thoughts exactly. I need some help."

"Name it and you got it."

C.J. knew that his friend would always come through. With their combined drug world connections they might be able to learn what was really going down. Fortunately, when a drug lord sneezed anywhere in the world, someone in American narcotics law enforcement responded with a gesundheit.

"I'll see what I can find out. But on to a bigger question. Has Selena moved back permanently or is this temporary?"

"I don't know." C.J. shrugged. "I guess I'd better tell Olivia, huh?"

"That's for sure."

"Problem is, I can't ever seem to get her alone. And this isn't a subject we can discuss at the Dairy Queen."

"Privacy would be good. So what do you want to do?"

C.J. took a sip of beer; it was a stalling tactic, but he had a big favor to ask. "Do you think you guys could invite her to dinner and then I could show up? Hopefully her manners will keep her from bolting."

Christian almost choked on his brew. "If we pull that, she's gonna be madder than an old wet hen. And you won't be the only one she'll want to hang." He paused as he thought. "When would we have to do this?"

"Sooner rather than later," C.J. said.

"That's what I was afraid of. Let me talk to Lolly and get her take on it."

C.J. clapped his friend on the back. "That's all I can ask. If that doesn't work out, I'll kidnap her. We know enough cop types to keep me out of trouble, don't you think?" He laughed and signaled the waitress for a refill.

"I'M NOT SURE this is a good idea," Lolly informed her husband as she flipped chicken in the skillet. "Livy probably won't speak to me for weeks. She specifically said she didn't want to have anything to do with C.J."

Christian was sitting at the kitchen table helping Amanda with her homework while idly pushing one twin in her wind-up swing. The other baby was sound asleep in a portable bassinet. Lately the twins had been colicky and the members of the Delacroix family were experiencing major sleep deprivation.

"I know. When you're talking about those two, I don't know which one is more obstinate. If they're ever going to get together, someone's gonna have to give them a big shove." He ran his fingers through his hair. "I just wish we hadn't been elected."

Lolly frowned and took the last drumstick out of the pan. "Me, too."

The squeak of the screen door announced Olivia's arrival. "Hey, it smells good in here."

Showtime!

"How's my favorite kid?" She kissed the top of Amanda's head.

"Guess what, Aunt Livy. I've been selected to dance around the maypole. And I get a new party dress and put flowers in my hair and everything. Isn't that cool?" Amanda exclaimed.

"Hey, that's great." Olivia looked at Lolly, who rolled her eyes. When they'd danced around the maypole in elementary school, Lolly got twisted up in the ribbons and fell on her rear in front of the all their classmates, the parents and half the citizens of Port Serenity.

"And how's my favorite bad guy?" She ruffled Christian's hair. He hated that particular show of affection, and that was why she did it.

Olivia leaned over the swing and tweaked the baby's cheek. "And how's our little snookums doin'?" There was something about a cute baby that made even the most intelligent woman revert to baby talk. She lifted the tiny foot, looking for a small indelible mark Lolly had put on Dana's foot to tell the girls apart.

"I'm using nail polish on their pinkies now. Pink's for Dana, red's for Renee. It seemed more sanitary than a Marks-a-Lot," Lolly said as she placed a glass of wine in front of Olivia. "Drink up. You're going to need it."

"What?" Olivia asked, but was distracted when Lolly spoke to her daughter.

"As soon as you finish your homework, you can scoot on over to Leslie's house."

"Yes, ma'am. I'm done." Amanda slammed the cover of her book closed.

"Give your mama some sugar." Lolly leaned down and Amanda obliged with a kiss before she skipped out the back door.

"Where's Bren?" Olivia asked.

"He has a date," Christian answered. "Tonight's the spring formal."

"Heaven help us all." Lolly sighed. "That boy is so handsome I almost cried."

"Almost?"

"Okay, I'll admit it. I cried." Lolly's admission was cut short when Marcela arrived.

She ignored the adults and went straight to the twin who wasn't sleeping. "Are you Mee Maw's little girl?" she asked and then gave the baby raspberry kisses. "I'll take Dana to the nursery and when Renee's awake up bring her on up. Sissy's coming over later and we're going to dye her hair. She wants to be a redhead. I swear that woman's nuts." She picked up the baby, then turned to Olivia. "You're looking lovely, as usual," she said and made a quick exit.

"Thanks, Mee Maw," Olivia called after her. Why was Marcela babysitting, if they were having a simple family dinner? Olivia's BS meter kicked in. Something was going on and she intended to find out what. As a matter of fact, Christian didn't look all that innocent, either.

"Okay, what's happening?"

Before either of her hosts could answer, another visitor made an appearance.

"They're doing me a favor."

Olivia would recognize that voice in the middle of a Shriners' convention. She'd been set up. And by her best friend, no less.

Olivia spun on Lolly. "Lavinia Lee Delacroix, I can't believe you did this. Especially after our little talk," she snapped. "And you!" She jabbed a finger at Christian. "Don't think I'll forget this."

"Mind your manners," Lolly interjected. "It's simply fried chicken, not a peace conference. So take this," she handed a platter of chicken to her friend, "and get your butt into that dining room before I have to hurt you."

"Humph." Olivia flounced off, the aroma of chicken wafting behind her.

C.J. put on a sheepish grin. "Uh-oh."

"Yeah, uh-oh. I'm just glad that girl doesn't have a scalpel with her. She keeps threatening to neuter someone and the thought of that…"

Both men cringed.

"Here." Lolly shoved a bowl of mashed potatoes at her husband. "And you." She pointed at C.J. "Take this bottle of wine and pour her a huge glass. I think we'll have to get her drunk."

Absolutely!

* * *

SEVERAL LARGE GOBLETS of Chardonnay, half a chicken and two pieces of pie later, Olivia was feeling no pain. What was it about tricky situations that made her ravenous? Not to mention light-headed and giggly. Darn it, the giggle bubbled up again. She pushed her goblet toward C.J. for a refill.

"Nope. That's it for you, little darlin'." He took her hand and held it. "And you're not about to drive home in your condition."

Flustered beyond belief, Olivia snorted. "I'll walk."

Lolly jumped into the conversation. "It's over five miles to your house. And if you put one foot out on the street, I'll arrest you for public intoxication."

"I'll have you know I am *not* drunk." She'd plead guilty to giddy or maybe even a bit tipsy, but not drunk. That was too common for words. "And you're not much of a friend." She didn't actually mean it; Lolly was closer than a sister.

Ignoring Olivia's remark, Lolly stood up to clear the table. "And this friend has a couple of babies who are going to wake up hungry, so C.J. will take you home." She pulled the end of Olivia's ponytail. "I don't want any guff off you. Christian will drive your car over in the morning." Lolly disappeared through the kitchen door with an armload of dirty dishes.

"I guess arguing won't make any difference, huh?" When another giggle bubbled up Olivia clapped a hand over her mouth.

It wasn't the right time to get arrogant, but C.J. was pretty sure he'd win this skirmish. The larger battle might be another story.

Christian collected the remaining dishes. "You guys need to talk, so why don't you make yourselves scarce."

"Right, boss." C.J. pulled out Olivia's chair and by sheer willpower refrained from kissing the back of her neck. She had such a kissable neck, but that would be a major tactical error. And in this war of wills he couldn't afford even a tiny blunder.

THE SANDY ROAD LED down to a spit of land facing the ocean. It wasn't that far from C.J.'s beach house, but it felt like a world away from the lights and activity of town. Thank goodness the teenage make-out crew hadn't discovered this little spot of paradise.

C.J. stopped the Explorer at the edge of the dunes. He stole a look at Olivia. If her back was any straighter he'd be tempted to check her for rigor mortis.

"What do you think you're doing?" she asked, and the temperature in the car dropped at least ten degrees. "I live on Mimosa Trail. If you don't remember, that's on the other side of town." She gave him her frostiest glare. "So fire up this car and take me home. Otherwise," she warned him, "I'll report you for unlawful imprisonment. So there."

His reaction wasn't exactly what Olivia wanted or expected. He chuckled. Darn it—the man chuckled!

"That does it!" She reached for the door handle,

but it was an official police car and he had full control of all the locks. "Damn it. Let me out of here."

"Oh, Livy, honey." He massaged the back of her neck. The disaster the summer before had been his fault and he wasn't about to repeat the mistake by keeping anything from her. Slowly but surely, he could feel her resolve weakening. By hook or by crook, that wall she'd built was about to tumble.

"There's something I have to tell you and I figured I'd better do it someplace you can't run away from me."

"So you dragged our friends into this mess? How dare you?"

"They both agreed I needed to talk to you. So yes, reluctantly they helped me."

Olivia maintained her glare. "If this is so earth-shaking, tell me and make it snappy. I need to go home to paint my toenails."

C.J. leaned over the console as far as he could. Although his range of motion was limited by the computer and police equipment, he did manage to slide the scrunchie out of her ponytail and run his fingers through the fall of satiny hair. "Before you hear it from someone else, I thought I'd tell you that Selena's back in town. She's staying at Mom's house."

Total silence.

"She thinks someone was following her in Dallas. It scared her so she came back to the only place that's ever felt like home. That hellhole she grew up in in Colombia was never more than a place to sleep.

Anyway, I've put out some inquiries to see if this has anything to do with her brother."

More silence.

He ran a finger down her delicate, but decidedly obdurate, chin. "When I brought her to this country, she became a member of our family, and part of the deal with family is safety and protection."

"Hmph!" she snapped, but then she mellowed. "Okay, I understand. But it doesn't make any difference between us. Selena, no Selena, it really doesn't matter. I still don't trust you." Especially in matters of the heart. After a lot of soul-searching Olivia had come to the realization that Selena was an innocent participant in the whole mess. The fact that C.J. hadn't loved her enough to tell her about Selena was the problem. "So, why don't you take me home?"

"Not until I do this." C.J. cupped her head and pulled her closer. He rubbed his lips back and forth, his tongue insistent on gaining entrance.

"Oh, boy," she muttered. Her ability to resist this guy was practically nonexistent.

That small concession allowed him to deepen the kiss. And kiss her and kiss her until reality, in the form of a piece of equipment imbedded in his side, broke the trance.

He leaned back and sighed. "First of all, I'm too old to neck in a car. And second, a police cruiser isn't exactly the most romantic place in town. But—" His admission was interrupted by a blast from the radio. The alarm at the Piggly Wiggly had gone off.

"I guess I should find out what's happening." He started the engine. "But I'll give you fair warning. This is far from over."

A DECADE BEFORE, Olivia's wedding fiasco had been the talk of the Port Serenity grapevine, so C.J. knew the basics. Corrine had provided the specifics. He realized that trust and abandonment were huge issues with Olivia. So his job was to prove he wasn't anything like her ex-fiancé. When he finally managed to get a ring on her finger, she'd know he wasn't going anywhere. In fact, he'd be impossible to ditch.

He was a *very* patient and tenacious man. Giving up wasn't in his nature.

Chapter Twelve

It had been two and a half very long days since "the abduction/seduction"—or whatever the heck it was that C.J. thought he'd been doing. Surely he didn't think she'd fall into his arms and tell him everything was just peachy.

Olivia hadn't seen hide nor hair of him—not at Piggly Wiggly or Daisy's Diner or even the courthouse. Not that she was lurking around that mausoleum of bureaucracy. The funny thing was, she hadn't seen Selena around town, either. So what did that mean?

And why couldn't she concentrate? Olivia slammed the huge medical book shut and rubbed her temples. She was deep in thought when the phone rang. It was Bren, Lolly's son.

"Hi, Bren honey. What's up?"

"Hi, Aunt Livy. The football team and the band are sponsoring the annual Bovine Bingo, and I wanted to see if you'd like to buy a ticket." He paused. "They're expensive, but the grand prize is a trip to the Caribbean."

Olivia was a sucker for a kid selling anything, so of course she'd buy a ticket, but she had to ask. "How expensive?"

"Twenty-five dollars. But the prizes are all super good. There's a big-screen TV and a weekend in San Francisco. Really neat stuff. How about it?"

"Sign me up. Do I get to select my own number?"

"Yep, unless someone else already has it."

"Then I want B-19. My birthday's the 19th and Mrs. Pomerantz, our resident bingo expert, claims that B numbers always come up."

Olivia could hear some papers rustling. He was obviously checking the availability of B-19.

"I can give you B-19 in the fourth round. We won't know until that night which round has the grand prize."

"I'm sure I'll be lucky." She meant that facetiously. Lady Luck hadn't been in her corner lately.

BOVINE BINGO HAD BEEN an annual May fund-raiser in Port Serenity since the 1940s. The kids solicited prizes, sold tickets all over town, and on the day of the big bash they painted a huge bingo card on the football field. It always turned into a citywide festival with food booths, craft vendors and games. At the end of the bingo, volunteers from the civic groups in town did a thorough pooper scoop, set up a temporary wooden dance floor and then everyone pulled on their boots and had a rip-roarin', good-time country-western dance.

Olivia and her mom and dad, Rose and Raul,

joined Lolly, Christian and the twins in the stands. "We haven't missed anything, have we?" she asked. "Daddy had to have another corn dog." She winked at her father.

Even at fifty-five Raul Alvarado was a remarkably handsome man—tall with dark wavy hair highlighted by silver and twinkling brown eyes.

"Nope, they haven't even brought out the cows yet." Lolly motioned in the direction of the end zone. "Amanda and Leslie are right in the middle of the action." One of the stars of Bovine Bingo mooed and tried to get away from its youthful handler.

"Amanda wants to join 4-H so she can have her own cow," Lolly said with an exaggerated sigh. "Heaven help us. What's wrong with a gerbil or a ferret? I might even consider a pony, but I absolutely refuse to keep a cow in my backyard."

When it came to famous last words, Olivia was sure that proclamation would one day rank as world-class.

Four well-fed cows were led out onto the field as the high school band blasted out "Old McDonald." Only in down-home America would productive college-educated members of society be shouting encouragement to a cow to "do its business" on a football field. But that was exactly what happened in Bovine Bingo. Poop on the right spot, and some lucky dude would win a plasma TV.

"This sure isn't Radio City Music Hall, is it?" Olivia observed.

"Nope, it's pure Texas. And I have O-63 in the

first round so hush up. My money's on Bessie."
Lolly's focus was on the huge white-faced Hereford
moseying over to the edge of the bingo card to find
better grazing. And everyone knew a happy cow was
a relaxed cow. "Go Bessie!" she shouted, then turned
to Olivia. "The prize for this round is a wide-screen
TV." About that time Bessie wandered over to the G
squares and plopped a big one on G-57. A shout
went up from the other side of the stadium. "Crumb.
I really wanted that TV."

"You still have a chance for one of the consola-
tion prizes," Olivia commented.

"Like I really want a six-month supply of bait
shrimp?"

"I'm going for tacos. You girls want anything?"
Raul asked.

"No, Daddy, I'm fine. How about you guys?"
Olivia asked the group in general. By this time
Marcela and Aunt Sissy had joined them. Olivia had
always thought of the sisters as the dynamic duo.

"Aunt Sissy, I love the red hair," Olivia said, and
realized she actually meant the compliment. There
was something about those sisters that defied age.

Christian pushed the baby carrier closer to Lolly.
Both twins were asleep—and that in itself was a miracle. "I'll go with you, Raul." He leaned over and
kissed Lolly. "I'll be back in a few minutes. You
want an ice cream?"

"Sure, chocolate with sprinkles."

The hooting and hollering continued unabated.
B-12 won a year's supply of oil changes at the Jiffy

Job. O-67 walked away with a weekend at the Sea-crest Inn in Corpus Christi.

"Lordy mercy, look at that." Lolly pointed at the end zone where the cows were grazing. Amanda was clutching one end of a halter while another teenager coaxed a Guernsey out on the field. "I can see it now. In a year I'll have Old Bossy as a permanent tenant. Just how long does a cow live if it doesn't become hamburger?" she asked Olivia. "And do you make house calls on large animals or would I have to buy a trailer?"

Olivia patted her friend's arm. "For you, I'll do a house call. And their life expectancy is about fif-teen years."

"Good heavens, in fifteen years Renee and Dana will be in high school."

Now that was something to think about. In fifteen years, Olivia and Lolly would be creeping up on fifty. *Madre de Dios!*

Olivia was contemplating middle age when the fourth round started.

"What's your number?" Lolly asked.

"B-19." Olivia turned her attention to the field. "I wasn't listening. What's the prize this time?"

"It's the Caribbean cruise for two," Lolly an-swered. "And—" she waved toward the field "—that big black-and-white bovine is wandering over to the B squares. Look, look, look!" She was gesturing at the cow grazing in the middle of the B-19 square.

"Do it, do it, do it," Olivia muttered, holding up her crossed fingers. "That's it, go for it." And sure enough, the cow complied. "Yes!" she squealed and pumped a fist in the air. "I'm off to the Caribbean." Olivia ran down to the field to claim her prize. The only time she'd ever been a winner was in junior high—and that was burgers for two at the Dairy Queen.

She handed the winning number to the announcer and sashayed out to the B-19 square, careful to avoid the unmentionables. Strappy sandals and cow leavings—yuck!

A voice boomed from the loudspeaker. "And the winner of our Caribbean cruise for two is…wait a minute." There was a long pause while Olivia fidgeted and waved to the audience.

"Uh-oh." The announcer cleared his throat. "Seems we have two winners. I'm not sure how that happened. At any rate, the winners are Dr. Olivia Alvarado and Sheriff C. J. Baker. Maybe they can take the trip together." A wave of chuckles rolled through the audience.

Olivia glared at C.J. as he sauntered out onto the field. How dared he horn in on her prize? When he joined her, she let him have it with both barrels. "How did you manage to rig it so this…this… this—" she waved a hand in the direction of the now grazing Jersey "—this cow did your bidding?" Okay, that sounded unreasonable, even to her ears.

His grin was so big that his dimple seemed cavernous. "Little darlin', even I couldn't manage that stunt. As for us both having the same number, it has to be a royal screw-up or some kind of great cosmic joke. Never seen it happen before."

"Hmph!" Great—she was reduced to monosyllabic comments. What was it about this guy that left her speechless? And what was with the duplicate numbers? Was her godson in on some matchmaking deal—no way, it had to be a big goof.

He tipped back his Stetson and grinned. "We could use it for our honeymoon."

"What?" That did it. He could have the cruise. She started to stomp off but he grabbed her arm and yanked her into his arms. Then right there, in front of the Port Serenity High School band and football team, the Chamber of Commerce and half the folks in town, he launched into a world-class lip lock while the audience hooted encouragement.

Much to Olivia's chagrin, her knees turned to Jell-O as she melted against him. This wasn't Dr. Olivia Alvarado, cum laude graduate of vet school, who clutched the back of his neck and wholeheartedly got into the spirit of the kiss. Absolutely not!

She'd never, ever, do anything like that. Especially not right in middle of B-19—that would be more common than pig tracks.

Chapter Thirteen

Olivia was involved in a therapeutic baking session. Chocolate had always been a great antidote for man trouble. Whenever she thought about necking with C.J. in front of half the town, she wanted to beat her head on a hard surface. She was necking with him—necking! Ye gods.

She was contemplating a primal scream when a tap on the back door heralded the arrival of a flurry of blond females.

"Hi, Aunt Livy. Mama and I are headed to Super Saver to get me a South Beach Barbie. Are you making chocolate chip cookies and can I have some dough?" The young dynamo dashed to the bowl, finger ready to sample the uncooked goodies.

"It's 'may I'; and you're not doing anything until you wash your hands," Lolly admonished. She made shooing motions toward the powder room at the front of the house.

"South Beach Barbie?" Olivia inquired as she took out a pan of cookies.

Before the chocolate morsels had a chance to cool Lolly found a spatula and lifted a cookie. "Chocolate chips *and* brownies?" She eyed the iced chocolate goodies. "Last time I remember you making cookies *and* brownies was when Dr. Taylor sold the vet practice and you thought you'd have to move to Corpus and work at the 24-hour emergency clinic. I don't suppose I have to ask what's got your knickers in a twist, do I?"

Olivia sat down and put her head in her hands. "No, I don't guess so. C.J. has me so discombobulated I don't know what to do. I can't believe I was kissing him in the middle of the football field. But I can't seem to help myself. Swear to goodness, whenever he lays a pinkie on me, my brain goes on vacation. And damn it all, he's sexy and adorable and funny."

Lolly chuckled, tried to stop herself and then reverted to a series of giggles. "Actually, I couldn't quite believe that kiss, either. I'm surprised you guys didn't singe the grass. And what did he say to you before he so graciously gave you the prize?"

Unable to come up with any good lie, Olivia shook her head. "He said we could use it for our honeymoon."

Her admission elicited another hoot of laughter. "That boy has the nerve of a riverboat gambler. Honeymoon! Wait till I tell Christian."

Olivia was about to tell her to back off; she wasn't in the mood for sarcasm. But the opportunity was lost when Amanda returned.

"Mama, look what I found in the bathroom. It would go great with my pig collection."

The child was holding the pink pig Florene had given Olivia as a hostess gift. She had forgotten she'd put it under the sink in the powder room.

"Amanda, you know better than to go snooping in people's private stuff."

"Yes, ma'am. I was just trying to find a towel."

Amanda seemed about to cry, so Olivia gave her a big hug. "That's okay, sweetie. I forgot I had it. It was so ugly I just stuck it away. Tell you what. Let me keep it a little while longer just to make sure Miz Hardaway doesn't want it back, and then it's yours." She glanced apologetically at Lolly. "That is, if it's all right with your mama."

"I guess that's okay." Lolly held her arms out for her daughter. "Now, thank your aunt Livy for bailing you out."

"Thanks, Aunt Livy. Can I…" She paused and started her sentence again. "May I have a cookie?"

"Sure enough." Olivia handed Amanda the plate. "You also need some for the road." She rummaged in the cabinet for a small plastic bowl. "Here you go." She put a dozen warm cookies in the container and snapped the lid shut.

Lolly stood to leave. "I had a purpose for coming by other than getting under your skin about C.J. and raiding your cookie jar. Mee Maw's been snookered into doing a Sara Belle bash and she needs all the warm bodies she can find."

"Oh, please. Isn't one party enough?"

"Definitely—but if you'll help out my mom, I promise we'll only stay for a head count and then I'll take you to dinner."

"Oh, all right." Olivia sighed in resignation—she knew she wouldn't win this one. Lolly had perfected her wheedling skills at a very young age and she wasn't the least bit shy about using them. "But I absolutely will not be a model." The episode with C.J. and the red teddy was indelibly imprinted on her memory. "And I am not a cheap date. I veto the Pizza Place."

"How about the Shrimp Shack?" Lolly named the fried-food mecca of Port Serenity.

C.J. LOOKED UP from the report he was studying. "What do you need, Harv?" His detective was standing in the doorway trying to get his attention.

"The Bayou Church has been vandalized. The office was tossed and they also hit the storage areas. Seems they did a pretty thorough search. I thought you'd want to know."

Church vandalism was rare in Aransas County. And the fact that it had happened at Brother Hardaway's church made it a bit more interesting. But one glance at the pile of folders on his desk and C.J. decided his deputies could handle the problem. That didn't stop him from asking about the investigation.

"And?" he asked.

"And you said to be on the lookout for anyone new or suspicious in town and I think this may qualify." The deputy paused for dramatic effect. "We have a couple of witnesses. Mrs. Pomerantz and Mrs. Schmidt were collecting cans from the church Dumpster."

"Good God, what were they doing Dumpster diving?" C.J. wanted to groan. "Go on."

"They saw two guys drive in on motorcycles and then pick the lock on the front door."

"I hate to even ask, but how did they know they were picking the lock?"

"I suspect they watch too much *Court TV*."

C.J. agreed with his deputy's assessment. "Did they by any chance give you a description of the suspects or provide any license plate numbers for the bikes?"

"They said one of the guys was the spitting image of Cesar Romero and the other one was so ugly his mama should have sent him back at birth. Plus they said neither of the dudes had helmets on. But they didn't get a plate number."

C.J. raised an eyebrow.

"Hey, boss." The detective held up his hands in surrender. "That's exactly what they said. And who is Cesar Romero?"

"Beats me."

Great—his only two witnesses were Dumpster-diving octogenarians.

THIS PARTICULAR CRIME had no connection with Selena, but it prompted C.J. to do some more research on her problem. He picked up the phone and punched in a number he knew well from his previous life.

After numerous clicks and several rings in a faraway country, a man answered. "Whatcha want?"

"I haven't seen you in five years and your phone manners haven't improved one bit."

"Neither have my table manners. How ya doin' there, old buddy?"

If they'd been face-to-face, his friend and informant would be slapping him on the back. "Not bad. I need a favor."

"Name it," the man said with certainty.

C.J. explained he was looking for information on Enrique Bolivar's whereabouts and activities—particularly in relation to Selena.

"I'll put my ear to the ground and let you know what I find out," his friend assured him and rang off.

His next plan of attack included a call to Christian.

"Have you learned anything about Bolivar?" C.J. asked. He was being abrupt, but he was antsy as hell.

"Nice to hear from you, too," Christian answered. "And no. I've put out feelers everywhere and I still haven't heard anything. Meet me tonight, say around six at the Shoreline, and we'll see if we can come up with a game plan."

"Sounds good to me." If, with all their contacts, they couldn't figure out what the guy was doing, he was probably up to no good. And that didn't bode well for Selena's safety.

CHRISTIAN WAS ALREADY at the bar when C.J. arrived for their strategy session. He pushed a basket of fried shrimp at his friend. "Here, you look like you could use some junk food."

C.J. picked up a shrimp. "Thanks, Dr. Delacroix. You probably think I need a beer, too."

"Yep," Christian replied and motioned to the waitress.

They waited until C.J. ordered and then got down to business. Even though they were familiar with most of the players in the drug underworld, they'd struck out on information other than some vague rumors. And if they planned to go head-to-head with Enrique Bolivar they had to have a whole lot more than idle gossip. Jeez!

Chapter Fourteen

C.J. had been mysteriously absent since the infamous night at the football field—not that Olivia had noticed. Yeah, right! She realized he was busy with the Selena situation and then there was the Bayou Church vandalism, but he *did* have a telephone. And speaking of phones, Olivia was updating her patient notes when hers rang.

"Hi, sweetie. Are you busy?" Rose asked.

"Hi, Mom. I'm finishing up my paperwork and then I have to check on a beagle with a broken leg. He ran out in front of a car."

"Oh, my. That poor driver must have been in a tizzy."

"She sure was. But it was sort of a case of the dog hitting the car instead of the other way around. And he'll be okay. We just want to keep him overnight." Olivia could hear loud conversation in the background. Uh-oh, it sounded like an Alvarado family get-together. "What's up?"

Rose lowered her voice. "Aunt Emelda is here and she brought Cousin Maria and her family. Your aunt is making enchiladas." Her voice was almost a whisper. "I'm desperate for moral support and your dad's holed up in the den watching bass fishing on TV. He's *no* help at all." Rose continued without pausing. "Can I tempt you with a big plate of enchiladas?"

That suggestion brought on a big sigh. She'd rather dine at a Greyhound bus station than face Aunt Emelda, but how could she refuse her mother's pitiful plea. "Okay. I'll be there in about an hour." When had Caspar Milquetoast taken over her body? She knew the word "no," really she did. But Aunt Emelda *was* the enchilada diva of south Texas.

The fragrant smell of Tex-Mex cuisine tickled her nose the minute she opened the front door. That welcome was immediately undone by the sounds of prepubescent discord coming from the living room. Cousin Maria was okay, but her four kids were little terrors. Between six and eleven in age, they could take "he touched me" and "she's looking at me" routines to an altogether new level. The latest screech had Olivia reevaluating the merits of the best enchiladas south of San Antonio.

She ducked into the den. Sure enough, her dad was in his Barcalounger, the TV blaring a Budweiser commercial. "Hi, Daddy." She hugged him around the neck. He had always been her hero. He was able to manage the park system of Port Serenity while keeping up with Rose, and that was no easy feat. But even *he* couldn't handle Aunt Emelda.

"I think your mother could use some reinforcements." He flinched visibly at the next high-pitched

scream. "The only reason she hasn't scalped those
kids is Aunt Emelda and *el mal ojo*." Olivia could tell
he really, really wanted to cross himself but refrained. Then he grinned. "I'm a chicken."

"Oh, Daddy, come on, get brave." Olivia picked
up the remote and turned off the TV. "If I have to go
in there, so do you."

OLIVIA HAD TO LEAN way down to kiss her great-
aunt's weathered cheek. "That was fantastic and I'm
stuffed. But I think I'll head home now." Emelda
Delgado was a five-foot-tall, roly-poly dynamo, and
as the matriarch of the family she was a force to be
reckoned with. Her religion was a quirky mixture of
Catholicism and mysticism, with a smidgen of
Mayan sun worship thrown in.

Emelda put her hands on Olivia's cheeks. "I want
you to bring the young man of your heart to see me.
He's a good person and he loves you." She peered into
Olivia's eyes. "There's danger out there, and it's looking for you. You must promise to be very careful."

Olivia suppressed a shudder. As much as she hated
to admit it, in her heart she believed that her relative
had the "sight." And when that woman decided to
brew up a love potion or even worse, a curse—watch
out!

Olivia was still thinking about Emelda's strange
warning when she drove out of her parents' gravel
driveway. Her folks lived in the south end of the
county because Mama liked the solitude and Daddy
loved the sound of the surf.

Tim McGraw was crooning on the CD player, she had a great car, the moon was high, her tummy was full of enchiladas and there was the slightest smell of brine in the air. Her only worry was Aunt Emelda's vague warning, but Olivia decided to think about that later.

C.J. WAS DRIVING HOME from his meeting with Christian when the radio crackled. The medics and a deputy had been dispatched to Ida Whitaker's house. Talk about a name that brought on a cold sweat. Mrs. Whitaker started teaching third grade around the time of the ice age, and she'd been the bane of his eight-year-old existence. After-school detention was almost standard operating procedure. He wasn't that bad—really!

C.J. whipped the Explorer around and headed straight to Mrs. Whitaker's house. Not that he cared what happened to the old battle-ax, but he was already in the neighborhood.

An EMT vehicle was parked in the driveway and the front door of the white clapboard house was standing wide open. A crescendo of barking almost drowned out the sound of voices.

Almost three decades ago, she'd been larger than life to C.J. Now she was a delicate white-haired woman in a pink nightgown. He could have run over her in the middle of town and not recognized her, but his former teacher knew him instantly.

"Cookie Baker, get in here and tell these *people* I'm not going to the hospital," she insisted.

Obviously age hadn't diminished her commanding voice. The attending deputy's grin was cut short by his boss's scowl.

C.J. kneeled by the gurney and tipped his Stetson. "Mrs. Whitaker, ma'am. Let me talk to these nice folks and find out what your problem is." He patted her arm.

The feisty octogenarian swatted his hand. "Don't be condescending to me, young man. Don't forget, I knew you when you thought blowing milk out your nose would impress the girls."

Busted! Stories about this conversation were going to run through the sheriff's office like wildfire.

"You mean it didn't?"

She swatted him again, affectionately this time. "You always were an annoying kid. Cute as a button, but a complete pain in the rear."

"Yes, ma'am." As an eight-year old his primary goal had been to create chaos and obviously he'd succeeded. But he was a grown-up now, and it was back to business.

He addressed one of the EMTs. "Hi, Jerry, what's up?"

"We think she has a broken hip, so we need to take her to the hospital."

"I'm right here, young man. Don't talk about me in the third person."

Thoroughly chastised, Jerry bowed his head. "Yes, ma'am."

"Now, Mrs. Whitaker, you really do need to let these folks help you."

"All right, all right." She waved one hand in the

air. "I'll go to the hospital. But you have to promise me you'll take care of Fluffy. My sister just went to the assisted living center, so I can't send my puppy to her." She tweaked C.J.'s cheek. "You're the only person I would trust with my baby."

"Yes, ma'am." Not that he had any intention of keeping a dog, not with his busy schedule. "I presume the barking is coming from Fluffy."

"Yes. He's such a sweetie. And I can't go off and leave him with just anyone. They might take him to the dog pound. But I have faith in you." Her eyes misted.

One of the medics cleared his throat. "Are we ready to go?" he asked.

C.J. was on the spot. The woman was obviously in pain and in need of medical attention. Plus it didn't look like she'd accept a *no*. "Tell you what. I'll take him for the time being. Then we'll figure out what you want to do. How's that?"

Mrs. Whitaker nodded as the barking grew more frenzied.

C.J. walked over and opened the door, freeing a tiny canine dervish. Fluffy jumped on the stretcher and bathed his mama's face in kisses.

He was a cute dog in a *fluffy* sort of way, but C.J. liked big, manly canine companions, and this little ball of white fur sported pink bows on his ears. Pink bows!

"Fluffy, listen to mama. Sheriff Baker will take care of you." Mrs. Whitaker was talking to the puppy as if he could understand. And darn it, the dog cocked his head and appeared to be listening.

"So you be a good boy." She shooed the dog off the gurney and the next thing C.J. knew, he had Fluffy in his arms.

Fluffy gave one swipe of his tongue over C.J.'s cheek and then settled down to be carried.

"No lickin', ya hear." C.J. felt the need to establish his alpha position. Unfortunately, it was already too late.

He and Fluffy watched the ambulance roar away. "Looks like we're stuck with each other, huh?" C.J. could swear the dog nodded, but that was silly.

C.J. deposited the dog on the passenger seat and sprinted to the other side of the car. After an exploration of the computer terminal and other assorted police equipment, Fluffy made himself at home and was snoring before C.J. put the Explorer in gear. C.J. could hear the Sonic beckoning, his snack of fried shrimp and beer a distant memory.

IT WASN'T UNTIL Fluffy jumped over the console and eyed C.J.'s burger that he realized he hadn't packed any of the dog's things. He didn't have any kibble, or a dish or a leash. And darn it, even the Super Saver was closed.

The dog's big brown eyes breached C.J.'s last line of defense, and there went half his burger. Then he shared a large order of cheese fries and a Frito chili pie with his new friend.

It wasn't until he was on the road that he heard the ominous tummy growls. Uh-oh. He'd screwed up—big time! The tummy rumbles continued, and when they were accompanied by noxious fumes C.J. realized that a patch of grass was his top priority.

C.J. was sitting on the curb contemplating his latest predicament when Olivia's 'Vette screamed into the parking lot and skidded to a stop. If he hadn't been dealing with a more pressing problem, swear to goodness, he'd have given that girl a speeding ticket.

THE EMERGENCY BAR on the top of the Explorer was the first thing that caught Olivia's attention. During the few seconds it took for her brain cells to fire, she almost passed the parking lot where C.J.'s car was sitting with the passenger door open. She spun into the lot and slid to a stop, oblivious to the fact that C.J. was on the curb watching the whole operation.

"Sweetheart, I should rescind your license. Do you ever drive that thing under the speed limit?" he drawled.

Irritated by the question, Olivia flounced over and joined him on the curb. "What are you—" Before she could finish the question she spied Fluffy who had finished his business and was nestled in C.J.'s lap. "And who is that?"

"This—" he held Fluffy up to face level "—is Fluffy. Against my better judgment, I'm his temporary guardian. You remember Mrs. Whitaker, our third-grade teacher, don't you?"

"Of course I remember her. I was her pet, unlike someone I know." She couldn't resist the jab.

"Yeah, and she never did discover that you filched my box of 64 Crayolas. Anyway, she broke her hip this evening and I temporarily inherited him."

Fluffy burped as he tried to reach Olivia's face for a big sloppy kiss. As a pet-lover she leaned forward to accommodate his show of affection.

"And please tell me why you're sitting on a curb holding Fluffy when it's way past everyone's bed-time?"

C.J. wrinkled his nose. "I'm trying to figure out how to clean that up." He pointed at the results of Fluffy's intestinal distress.

Olivia couldn't help her hoot of laughter—her misgivings about C.J. temporarily forgotten.

"I think maybe it was something he ate," C.J. admitted.

"And what did he eat?"

"Half a hamburger, most of a Frito pie and a bunch of cheese fries."

She snickered again. "What in heaven's name are you doing, feeding junk food to a dog. His bowel habits won't be normal until he expels it all from his system."

C.J. dropped his head in his hands. "Great, just freakin' fantastic." He gave Olivia his sexiest grin. "Could I convince my best vet friend to come out to my house and get him settled? I promise I'll be good." To seal the promise he gave his best Boy Scout salute. "Honest, I'm desperate."

Against her better judgment, Olivia decided to take pity. "Do you have any kibble?"

"Nope."

Olivia shook her head—men could be so clueless. "Follow me to the clinic so I can pick some up. Then we'll go to your place. And C.J., I swear to goodness if you try anything funny, you'll live to regret it."

Honest to God, she tried her best to be scary, but C.J. wasn't buying it.

"Scout's honor, I'll be good." He didn't bother to tell her he hadn't been a Boy Scout.

Chapter Fifteen

Olivia unloaded a dog bed, a bag of chew toys, a sack of dog food, a leash and two stainless steel bowls from the trunk of her car. "Don't just stand there, come and help me," she instructed. C.J. was holding Fluffy and watching the operation.

He surveyed the growing pile of canine equipment. "He's not spending the rest of his life here. As soon as Mrs. Whitaker is well, this guy's going home." When he held Fluffy up, he was rewarded with a face full of puppy kisses. "Jeez, I wish he'd stop that." C.J. wiped his mouth with the back of his sleeve.

Olivia laughed at the disgust on his face. "He loves you. And regardless of how long he's going to be a visitor, he has to have some basics." She picked up the wicker dog bed and pillow. "Plus, we need to get some medicine down him before he has to do his business again."

"Right," C.J. quickly agreed, even as he continued his staring match with the canine. After he was the first to blink, C.J. grabbed some more of the equipment and marched up the stairs to the wraparound porch. He'd been outstared by a *dog*.

"Nice place," Olivia commented as she trailed behind. "I'd love to have a house on the beach."

C.J. unlocked the front door and turned on the lights. "It needs a lot of work and that's why I could afford it. Actually, what it really needs is an interior decorator."

Boy, was he right about that. It was a study in '70s retro, down to the orange shag carpet. Olivia's fingers itched to slap on a coat of paint and rip out the hideous floor covering. "I guess you don't have time to get into a house remodel, huh?"

"Nope. I'm pretty busy these days." C.J. and Fluffy had retreated to the kitchen, where the human half of the duo was trying to convince the canine that a nap would be a good idea.

"Just give him some water," Olivia suggested. "Tomorrow morning you should give him a small bit of plain white rice and cottage cheese. If he tolerates that, you can increase the amount. For now, I'll give him a little something to help settle his intestines." She pulled a large bottle of Pepto-Bismol out of her bag and gave the patient a puppy-size dose.

Apparently all the excitement had put Fluffy in a mellow mood. He licked the remaining pink liquid off his furry lips, gingerly sniffed the bed, made three big circles of his accommodations, gave a Great Dane–sized burp and plopped down, falling into a deep sleep almost instantly.

"Puppies do that," Olivia commented. "I'll bet in

the middle of the night you find him on your bed with his head on your pillow."

There was a certain dark-haired beauty C.J. would rather have in his bed with her head on his pillow, but for the moment he'd give those lascivious thoughts a rest. After all, he had given his word. She'd said no funny business! So he'd better find something else to do with his mind—and his hands.

"Can I interest you in a glass of wine?" He opened the refrigerator door and held up an unopened bottle of white wine. "I also have some Cokes and a couple of Coronas." It had been a long time since C.J. had entertained, so the selection was sparse.

Wine wasn't the best idea in the world, especially considering Olivia's last encounter with the grape at Lolly's house, but it would take the edge off. "I'd love some wine." C.J. really did look cute fumbling around in the kitchen drawer for a corkscrew. Could he be domesticated? Or trusted? And why did it matter?

"What kind of dog do you think he is?" C.J. pointed the corkscrew at Fluffy. "Mrs. Whitaker said he's a poodle, but he's not shaped like any poodle I've ever seen." The ersatz poodle opened one eye, but apparently he didn't think the conversation was worthy of his attention, so he fell back asleep.

Olivia studied the pooch. "He looks like a bicha-doodle to me."

C.J. handed her a glass of wine. "And that sounds like a bunch of bull to me."

Olivia took a sip and laughed. "I'm pretty sure

he's mostly bichon frise with a little bit of poodle thrown in. Plus, he has a Jack Russell attitude. It's that big dog personality in a little dog body. I think he's adorable."

If only she thought *he* was adorable. "Let's go out on the deck." C.J. drew her out onto the wide wooden porch. The only sounds were the soft lull of the waves and the electronic zap of his mosquito terminator when an errant insect trolled too close. He lit several citronella candles as another line of defense.

"Have a seat." He indicated the two chaise longues. "Do you want a snack? I could probably scare up some crackers."

Olivia was encouraged by the fact that he seemed almost as nervous as she felt. There were so many things to discuss. Their relationship, Selena, trust, their relationship… Lord, was she obsessed or what? She really couldn't continue with the status quo— C.J. always touching her and nuzzling her and kissing her. Something had to be done.

So going by the theory that a good offense beat a better defense, she pressed on. "I guess it's time for us to have a talk, huh?" Olivia tried for casual but was afraid she might have failed miserably. Her mouth was as dry as the Sahara, but gulping the wine was a *really* bad idea.

C.J. rested his elbows on his knees and twirled the stem of his glass. "Since my goof in not explaining Selena is at the root of our problems, do you want me to tell you about her?"

"No. Yes. I don't know."

He smiled at her ambivalent answer. "It's a long story." He explained how he had met Selena at her brother's mountain fortress. "Selena learned English through *Brady Bunch* reruns. And she was smart enough to know what her brother had in mind, so she kept herself dressed like an urchin kid. You've seen her. It wasn't a very believable disguise and some of the hard-core bad guys were trying to force the issue. It was only a matter of time before someone raped her, so I decided to get her out of there."

C.J. described how he'd spirited her out of Bolivar's clutches and hidden her until he could work out the bureaucratic tangle of getting her into the U.S. "Christian, the captain and I called in every marker we had to make that deal." He shrugged, recalling the operation. "And even to this day, I'm sure if Enrique Bolivar discovers where she is, he'll pull every trick in the book to kidnap her and get her back. He thinks she's that valuable a commodity. And believe me, that's all she is to him—a possession. But she's like my little sister and I'll protect her with my life."

"Why didn't you tell me this before we got involved?"

That was a good question. Why hadn't he put everything on the table? The simple answer was he didn't know if Olivia would understand and he didn't want to jeopardize their fledgling relationship. Yet by not being completely honest he'd learned a valuable, but incredibly painful, lesson. When it came to dealing with women, particularly Olivia, honesty was the best policy. And how did he explain that without digging himself in even deeper?

"I love you and I didn't want to lose you," he answered as sincerely as he could.

Olivia had never thought of herself as a hearts-and-flowers kind of girl, but these were the most romantic words he could have said. And they were probably the *only* words that would have softened her heart, although she did intend to keep that very tender organ well protected. "Oh, honey, you wouldn't have lost me." She moved next to him on the chaise and ran her fingers through his shaggy, sun-kissed hair. "You did the only thing an honorable person could have done. What I'm having a hard time accepting is the fact that you didn't tell me."

He gave her one of his world-class smiles. "How about if I promise to always be completely honest with you, even if you ask me whether your dress makes your butt look fat." With that comment, his dimple made a surprise appearance.

Olivia launched herself at him, fighting a bout of giggles. Oops! Considering the fact she was now trapped beneath his long, lean body, that bit of silliness had turned into a major error. A delicious miscalculation.

"You know what, little darlin'? I think I fell in love with you way, way back when you first became the coroner, and you were bein' all official." He traced her lips with his tongue. "You were so prickly and feisty I couldn't resist." Then he dipped his head and kissed from her collarbone to the deep V of her cleavage.

Holy moly! It was a good thing she wasn't standing; her legs wouldn't have held her up.

"And I've wanted to do this for months." C.J. gently removed the clip holding her ponytail and ran his fingers through her hair. "It feels so good." The velvety strands sifted through his fingers as he held it up to his face and rubbed like a cat—a big sexy tomcat. "You're so beautiful," he sighed, and started a foray of kisses from her neck, to the delicate swirl of her ear, and across her cheek to the corner of her lips, and then back, bypassing her lips to start again on the other side.

The damn man was driving her crazy with lust. "Kiss me," she demanded and pulled his head down to feast on his sexy, sexy lips.

When C.J. came up for breath, he gave her another of his patented bad-boy grins. "That's what I like, a woman who knows what she wants." He chuckled. "Especially when she wants my body."

"Shut up and kiss me," she muttered, pulling up his T-shirt. She wasn't sure how it had happened, but her brain had disconnected and her body was fully in charge. She was lost, lost, lost. She was savoring the contrast between the crispy hair on his chest and the smooth skin of his back and reveling in his unique smell, which was both masculine and clean. She'd never be able to smell Irish Spring soap again without having a hot flash.

The tornado of emotions was hot and primitive but gentle and infinitely satisfying.

Uh-oh—there were too many clothes in this equation. Time for him to ditch the jeans, although the way he was intimately nestled between her legs and the friction of that denim was extremely erotic. They were pelvis to pelvis, and he was kissing her with a feverish intensity. And kissing wasn't all he did with a feverish intensity. No, sirree.

Chapter Sixteen

Olivia awoke with a start. It was the nightmare again. That nightmare where she was standing at the altar in a long white dress and everyone in town was watching and waiting—while her heart broke into a thousand little pieces. Without a groom, there wouldn't be a wedding, and in every one of those dreams the groom was missing in action. Just like it had been in real life.

Before Olivia opened her eyes she knew she'd made a terrible mistake. With C.J.'s hand resting on her waist and a hairy leg thrown over hers, escape would be tough but staying wasn't an option. Damn it—the sun wasn't up and she was trying to figure out how to sneak out like some kind of thief. Men!

A STREAM OF SUNLIGHT on his face brought C.J. out of an erotic dream featuring Olivia. He rolled over as something wet and cold nuzzled his neck and then went for his lips. That had possibilities, but what was with the wet-and-cold bit? C.J. cracked open one eye and discovered a black nose accompanied by two button eyes and a wet pink tongue.

"Yech!" He wiped a hand over his lips. "You have dog breath." Fluffy was his only bed partner, and probably had been for quite a while. Where was Olivia? Crap. He was obsessed with the most stubborn and skittish woman in south Texas. Talk about a recipe for heartburn.

"And you." He pointed a finger at the dog. "Your new name is Fang. Get used to it, because I'm not sharing my house or my car with anyone named Fluffy." C.J. stood up and stretched. "And since I obviously don't have anything better to do this morning, I'm off to the office and you're going with me."

Fluffy pranced to the end of the bed and perked up his ears.

SINCE OLIVIA WAS on weekend call, she went back to the clinic after she had "escaped" from C.J.'s house. When her rounds were finished she headed over to her parents' house. Normally her first choice for girl talk would be Lolly, but the Delacroix family was in San Antonio.

"Hi, Mom. That smells great." Bacon was sizzling in the pan and a fresh pot of coffee was brewing. It was a typical Sunday breakfast at the Alvarado house.

Rose's intuition took over almost immediately. "Oh, baby, what's the matter?" She turned off the stove and slipped an arm around her daughter. "Sit down and I'll make you some tea. Then you can tell me why you hightailed it over here on a Sunday morning, without even trying the old 'I want pancakes' excuse." Rose bustled to the stove and put on the kettle. Tea and sympathy were an age-old Irish tradition.

"Oh, Mama." Olivia rested her head in her hands. "I did something incredibly stupid."

Rose didn't comment as she dropped two tea bags into the teapot.

"I spent the night with C.J."

Rose covered the teapot with a quilted cozy and sat down.

"And I think I love him," Olivia cried. "I know it's stupid, and I probably need therapy, and I know it's the reason I'm going to end up an old-maid cat lady, but I can't seem to get past the Brian fiasco. Aaahh!" she screeched. "Why can't I just trust C.J.? One hundred percent wholeheartedly trust him."

Rose patted her shoulder. "Oh, Livy, sweetheart." She ran a hand down Olivia's hair. "C.J. isn't Brian. Swear to God, if I had Brian here right now I'd kill him."

Just the thought of her fiery, protective mother doing bodily harm to her ex-fiancé brought a smile to Olivia's face.

"Did I tell you he called me the other day?" Olivia asked.

"No, you didn't."

"I still don't know what he wanted. He just sort of beat around the bush. You know, typical Brian BS."

"Hmm."

"He did tell me he divorced his second wife."

Again Rose responded with a noncommittal *hmm*.

"He has a vet practice in Houston, so if you want to go up there and slap him around, I wouldn't object."

"I'll think about it. Although I doubt he's worth the effort. Now pour us both a cup and tell me why you're here and not at C.J.'s beach house."

That was a good question, and not one that Olivia could easily answer.

"DON'T EVEN SAY IT," C.J. advised the desk sergeant. The fact that he was at work on a Sunday morning was nothing unusual, but this time he was accompanied by a prancing white dog with pink bows on its ears. "His name is Fang, and he's here because I can't leave him at home alone." His tiny companion was madly wagging his tail. "He used my couch as a snack while I was in the shower. No telling what he'd do if I left him for eight hours."

"Do you have any chew toys?" the desk sergeant asked.

C.J. nodded. He had a whole bag of the worthless things.

"Didn't work, huh?"

C.J. shook his head.

"Then why don't you get one of those big cow leg bones down at the butcher shop. My Doberman thinks he's died and gone to heaven when he gets one."

Great, just what he needed—his sissy little lapdog gnawing on half a steer. "Thanks, I'll consider it." C.J. strolled back to his office and threw himself into his chair.

Weekends usually provided a quiet opportunity to do paperwork, but this Sunday was different. He couldn't stop thinking about his incredible night with Olivia. And damn it—why had she scooted out of his place as if it was on fire? With that woman, it was one step forward and ten steps back.

Fang had settled into an old leather chair and was snoring like a linebacker—at least *someone* was comfortable. Before C.J. could start on the pile of folders littering his desk, the phone rang. "Hey, boss. There's someone out here you're gonna want to see."

"And how do you know that?" At the moment C.J. wasn't in the mood to see anyone, not unless she was tall, sexy and had a ponytail.

"It's your brother, Chandler."

C.J. threw down the phone without even answering. His brother was supposed to be in Iraq working as a photojournalist. And if he wasn't where he was supposed to be, something was terribly wrong.

He sprinted down the hall and threw open the door. Crap! His normally robust brother was thin, almost to the point of being gaunt, and he was leaning on a cane. C.J. rushed out and wrapped Chandler in a bear hug. "What the hell are you doing here?" That wasn't very diplomatic, but diplomacy wasn't a big part of their relationship—the brothers were more into the rough-and-tumble, slap-on-the-back kind of love.

They were unmistakably similar in looks. They had

the same tall broad-shouldered build and blond hair. But where C.J. had a cocky charming persona, Chandler was darker, more sensual and introspective—the stereotype of a globe-trotting photojournalist.

Chandler pointed toward the door with his cane. "Let's go back to your office. I have a lot to tell you before I let Mom know I'm here."

That didn't sound good. Added to the fact that his brother appeared to have been on the losing end of a ten-round bout with George Foreman, and things were not looking sunny.

Chandler lost his grim expression when he spied Fang. The dog simply opened one eye, sniffed and fell back to sleep. "Don't tell me that mutt belongs to you."

"His name is Fang and he's a trained watchdog."

Chandler laughed in response to C.J.'s claim.

"And if you believe that, I've got some swamp land for sale. Have a seat. You have a lot of 'splaining to do." C.J. said as he perched on the edge of his desk. "And why didn't you let someone know when you were injured? That really pisses me off!"

Chandler studied the tips of his boots. "Initially I didn't want Mom to worry, and then I thought I'd be up and ready to go in a matter of days. Guess I was wrong, huh?"

C.J. poked his brother's shoulder. "You dumb jerk. There's e-mail, the fax, and gee—" he picked up the phone receiver "—even in the sticks we have this thing called a telephone. Plus I know how to keep my mouth shut." He rounded the corner of his desk and sat down. "So, what happened and what's the prognosis?"

Chandler explained that he'd followed a marine unit into a firefight and been blown against a wall when a car bomb detonated. Fortunately no one had been killed—unfortunately his back was all messed up. "Damn it! I would've been better off getting shot. At least they could've taken out the bullet and I'd have healed. With this they're not sure what's wrong or exactly what to do about it. I had surgery in New York, but it still hurts to sit, or stand, or walk or just about anything that requires motion." He shook his head. "I thought I'd come here and rest up for a while."

"When Mom finds out you'll need an undertaker, not a doctor." Without a doubt, Corrine Baker was going to be livid that he hadn't told her.

"The pain's better since my surgery, but my mobility sucks. The docs in New York told me I need extensive physical therapy."

"This gets better and better. Mom really *is* going to kill you, you know that?" C.J. sighed. "You had surgery in this country and didn't bother to call?"

"I know. That was stupid, wasn't it?"

"Yep," C.J. agreed, and wondered how to tell his brother about Selena. For some unknown reason, Chandler and Selena were like oil and water. And now they were going to be housemates. Oh boy, this would be mighty interesting.

"Selena is temporarily staying at Mom's." C.J. tried for a casual tone.

"Selena!" Chandler exploded. "What is *she* doing here?"

"Long story, but I'm afraid Enrique Bolivar has discovered she's in Texas."

"Some drug lord is looking for her and you sent her to live with our *mother*!" Chandler thumped his cane on the floor.

"In case you've forgotten, big brother, our mother can hold her own on the target range. She's aware of the danger, and I keep a close eye on them." He raised an eyebrow. "As a matter of fact, I'm glad you're back. We'll be better prepared, if Enrique tries to pull anything."

"Thanks. I'll just lie in bed and use your old rifle to pick off the bad guys as they break down the door. I'll be a sniper in rehab." Chandler chuckled. He stood and reached over the desk to shake hands with his sibling. "You've always been able to make me laugh."

If C.J. hadn't been afraid of hurting his brother, he would've initiated the poking and jabbing routine characteristic of their youth. Instead he came around the desk and slapped Chandler on the back. "Don't worry, you're tough. You'll get through this."

"LORD IN HEAVEN, what are you doing here?" Corrine Baker rushed down the steps of the family home and met C.J. and Chandler on the sidewalk. Chandler was at least eight inches taller than his mother, but Corrine still managed to give him a big hug. "What is this?" She tapped on his cane, but before he could answer, Corrine turned on C.J. "And why didn't you tell me your brother was coming home?"

C.J. shrugged. This was Chandler's problem. He had enough troubles of his own.

His contemplation was interrupted by a feminine voice. "Well, well. If it isn't the prodigal son." In a normal situation Selena was one of the nicest people around, but when she went up against Chandler she morphed into an A-1 shrew.

"And if it isn't Little Miss Jail Bait." Apparently absence hadn't made the heart grow fonder.

"I see that war hasn't improved your personality." Selena flounced into the house, slamming the front door with a resounding bang.

SHE PEEKED AROUND the curtain to view the family reunion on the front lawn. The Bakers (or at least C.J. and Corrine) had embraced her as if she was a long-lost relative. But there was something about Chandler that put every one of her warning signals on high alert. And as a carryover from her unorthodox childhood, Selena never ignored the prickle factor. God forbid it could be some kind of sexual attraction. The man would rather have his nails ripped out than hand her a compliment, or a smile, or even a kind word. Nope—this was hostility, pure and simple.

Selena was the resident expert on animosity. Her family made the Manson gang look like saints. Papa and brother dear were drug lords. Or at least they had been until Enrique sent Papa on a premature trip to some very, very hot place in the great beyond. And her mother—well, needless to say she'd disappeared from the picture well before Selena was out of diapers.

Childhood had been hellacious, and then when Selena hit puberty, the situation went from bad to worse—until C.J. provided her with a new life, and for that extraordinary act of kindness she'd be eternally grateful. So she'd grit her teeth, mind her manners and be cordial to Chandler even if he was a surly cretin.

And, she thought a bit perversely, a smile and a kind word would be the perfect way to drive him crazy.

Chapter Seventeen

After C.J. left Chandler to deal with Corrine and Selena, he wanted to do something about the situation with Olivia. In a fit of inspiration, he decided to proceed with the great romance caper.

Courting was like any type of major operation—the key was to formulate a strategy, organize it well and then march right in. In this little war of the heart nothing was off limits, not even Olivia's favorite bicha-doodle.

And that was how he found himself in the deserted parking lot of the vet clinic mulling over his next step. Go in—don't go in. Yes, no. Since when had he turned into a lily-livered coward?

"Ready, Fang?"

Fang hopped up on the console and panted in anticipation.

C.J. tried to untie Fang's bows. Police dogs shouldn't be sporting ribbons—it just wasn't manly. "Jeez, these things have to go." After another tug, C.J. realized he needed a pair of scissors, so he went on to a more important task.

"Do you think it's time to make our move?" he asked his canine friend, who responded with an enthusiastic yip.

"This is unbelievable. I'm reduced to asking a dog for advice." C.J grabbed both his Stetson and the puppy.

The receptionist was gone, but Olivia's 'Vette was still in the parking lot, so C.J. assumed she was in the back of the clinic.

"Olivia, are you here?" he called out as he rounded the reception desk and went through the doors marked Authorized Personnel Only. He'd bet he could get authorized if he put his mind to it.

Frenzied barking erupted from the occupants of cages lining the room, but Fang was oblivious to the noise.

"Olivia," C.J. called again, not at all sure anyone could hear over the racket. On second thought, this might not be such a good idea. He was about to make a retreat when Olivia appeared in an adjacent doorway.

"What are you doing here?" she demanded.

Uh-oh, not a good start. "Fluffy, um, Fang isn't feeling too well. So I thought I'd see if you'd give him a little checkup."

She tapped a lacquered fingernail on her teeth. "I suppose you didn't know we make appointments for that sort of thing, did you?"

C.J. managed to look sheepish.

The man should consider a career in acting. "And from just a cursory glance, I'd say your puppy seems fine."

Almost in confirmation, Fang climbed C.J.'s chest to give him a sloppy kiss.

"Yeah, well, appearances can be deceiving. Here." He thrust the dog into Olivia's arms.

"This is so lame. Aren't you even a tiny bit ashamed to use a poor innocent dog in your—" she waved her hands in the air "—scheme, or whatever."

"Nope." He grinned and his darned dimple looked too cute. "Can't say I am."

"All right, all right," Olivia conceded with very little grace. "You are the most tenacious man around, you know that?"

"Yes, ma'am. That's part of my charm."

Olivia resisted a snort as she carried Fang back to the examining room. After she'd checked the pup from stem to stern, she glared at C.J. "I told you he was fine. So why are you really here?"

He managed to look sheepish again.

"I really did want to have him examined, but I also wanted to see if you'd go to dinner with us."

"C.J., I, uh, I really don't think that's a good plan." She looked down at the floor, a move that turned out to be a tactical error because before she knew it, he was close enough for her to see the flecks of blue in his green eyes. "Last night was a huge—"

He took her in his arms. "Don't even consider saying it was a mistake," he admonished. "Making love with you was fantastic. At least, for me it was." Discussing feelings was well out of his comfort zone, but this time it seemed right. "Please, Olivia, let's have dinner and talk." Frankly he'd rather have a root canal than have a heart-to-heart discussion, particularly about relationships. But he was a desperate man—and desperate men were experts at groveling.

"And where could we take a dog to dinner?" she asked.

"I have an idea."

She just bet he did. And Lord only knew what kind of screwball plan he had up his sleeve. But Olivia could feel her resolve weakening, and a smart girl always knew when to concede. "Okay, but I have to clean up first." She sniffed her hands. "I smell like a dog. Why don't you and Fluffy go out front?"

"His name is Fang." C.J. pulled the dog's lips back, baring his teeth. "See, doesn't he look vicious?"

"Nope," Olivia responded with a laugh. "There are some balls and stuff in a basket under the bench. They should keep *Fang* busy. I'm not sure what'll entertain you. So scram. I'll be out in about fifteen minutes."

OLIVIA WAS TRYING to accomplish in a sink what should be done in a shower. More than likely it was a futile effort, but after a full day of wrestling dogs and cats she had some major repairs to accomplish. Off came the T-shirt and jeans.

"Whew." She flapped her clothes in an unsuccessful attempt to get rid of the animal fur and quickly decided it was a lost cause.

The locker in her office provided a limited wardrobe selection. It was either a pair of jeans or a black sequined cocktail dress. And she didn't think this was a "little black dress" event.

So she was stuck with jeans, a T-shirt with Texas Rose emblazoned on it in sequins, and a pair of strappy high-heeled sandals. Breaking bread with Mr. Sexy was a bad idea, so she told herself, so it really didn't matter what she was wearing.

"WHERE ARE WE GOING?" she asked for the fifth time and still didn't get an answer. Fang had made himself at home in her lap and was snoring like a stevedore. "And how can this dog make that much noise?" she asked.

C.J. glanced her way and chuckled. "Beats me. You're the vet. And I am planning to feed you. It just may not be what you're expecting."

Considering that there weren't any restaurants this far out of town, Olivia had almost decided they'd be dining at the Food World deli section.

But no—a supermarket wasn't his intended destination. It was a church. Good grief! They pulled into the crowded parking lot of the new Methodist church.

Olivia raised an eyebrow. "The church?"

"Yep. They're having a spaghetti feed and I promised Mom I'd show up." He hopped out of the Explorer and went around to the passenger door.

He took Fang from her lap and deposited him on the ground. "Rumor has it Mrs. Throckmorton's made her world-famous homemade strawberry ice cream."

What a bribe! Mrs. T was the best ice-cream

maker in south Texas. Baptist tacos were better than Methodist spaghetti, but even the Catholic fish fry couldn't beat Mrs. Throckmorton's icy delight.

Olivia jumped out of the SUV. "What are you waiting for?" She strolled into the church basement with Fang right behind her. The dog had major self-confidence!

C.J. chuckled but his amusement didn't last long. The first person he saw was Selena in all her red-haired splendor. Although Olivia claimed she wasn't mad at his ex-wife, he had his misgivings about an actual face-to-face meeting. Women could be so unpredictable.

"Let's head over to the dessert table." He laid a hand on Olivia's back and steered her away from the female members of his family, who were dishing up plates of spaghetti. He was beginning to think his idea might win an award for stupidity. If his brain had been engaged, he would've realized Selena would be here.

"Let's go straight to the ice cream. That way we can get some before it's all gone," he suggested.

Although Olivia seemed skeptical, she didn't object. Homemade ice cream *was* about as close to heaven as a girl could get.

Before they made it fifteen feet, several of C.J.'s constituents waylaid them, all wanting to chat, and as an elected official, he felt an obligation to meet and greet.

"Young man!"

C.J. held his breath. That voice could only belong to Mrs. Pomerantz.

"What have you found out about those dead bodies at the nature preserve?" Mrs. P. obviously had her hearing aid turned off and every word equaled the decibel level of a Stones concert.

He resisted the urge to stick his fingers in his ears and instead trotted out his best charm. "Yes, ma'am, it looks like they were accidental deaths." He winked at the octogenarian. He avoided adding that the police didn't have a clue about their identities—and God only knows, C.J. had tried and tried and tried to find out.

John and Jane Doe weren't on any missing persons' lists. C.J. had almost burned up the office fax machine following that dead-end trail. Plus, he wasn't any closer to finding out who'd dumped them at the nature preserve or why. The whole incident gave him a bad feeling.

"And isn't that Ida Whitaker's little dog, Fluffy?" Mrs. Pomerantz boomed.

The pooch in question had taken up residence on C.J.'s boot.

"Yes, ma'am. I'm keeping him until Mrs. Whitaker gets out of the hospital."

"Well, sonny, you might have a long wait. I hear Ida's thinking about going to the retirement home, and they don't allow animals. Didn't she call you?"

Ye gods! C.J. looked down at the canine menace who was chewing on his favorite lizard-skin Tony Lama boots. "Stop that." He shook his foot slightly, but failed to dislodge the pooch. He hadn't checked his home answering machine today.

"Are you sure?" he asked, even though he *really* didn't want to hear the answer.

"Absolutely," Mrs. Pomerantz pronounced.

"Gladys talked to her this morning. Ida's right happy you're taking such good care of her baby." She pinched his cheek before she strolled off.

Olivia was obviously trying to stifle a full-blown belly laugh.

"Don't you dare say anything."

She controlled the giggles, but couldn't squelch her grin.

"You'd better move your foot," she commented.

C.J. gasped. Fang had lifted his leg!

"Good Lord!" He picked up the dog. "Stop that. Do not, I repeat, do not chew on my boots, my car upholstery or my couch. And absolutely do *not* piss on my leg. You hear me?"

Olivia couldn't suppress another bout of giggles.

"And you…" He went nose-to-nose with Port Serenity's favorite vet. "I need help."

Instead of providing sage advice, Olivia cupped her hands around the dog's face and made kissy noises. "Is Daddy yelling at Snooky Wookums?"

"Come on." He took Livy's arm and steered her toward the exit. "Let's go to the Sonic."

"If you're treating, I want a double chili cheeseburger, ranch fries and a chocolate shake."

"You're on." C.J. laughed in spite of himself. "Damn, I like a woman with an appetite. You—" he ruffled Fang's ears "—are not having a jalapeño cheeseburger." He fingered one of the bows. "Next time I'm near a pair of scissors, remind me to cut these damn things off. A sheriff can't ride around with a dog wearing *bows*."

Chapter Eighteen

The situation wasn't working out the way C.J. had hoped. The good news was that Olivia was in his car. The bad news was that she was playing with the darned dog. C.J. might be down for the count but he certainly wasn't out of the game. For his next romantic skirmish, he thought he might try a candle-light dinner and roses. That would certainly be a world away from dinner al fresco at the Sonic.

"Are you ready to go?" he asked, as he put the remnants of his meal on the tray attached to his car window.

"Sure." Olivia handed him her trash while Fang made a circle in her lap and burped.

"You didn't feed him anything, did you?" C.J. wasn't sure he could take a repeat of Fang's previous encounter with a fast-food burger.

"Are you kidding me? I'm a professional. I wouldn't do anything *that* stupid."

Meaning he would—that was insulting, but if the crime fit and so forth.

C.J. was strategizing his next move when they drove past the darkened Bayou Church of the Saved Sinners. If it hadn't been for a sudden movement, he wouldn't have noticed the motorcycles by the stand of live oak. C.J. slowed the Explorer to check out the parking lot.

"What do you think is happenin' over there?" He pulled onto the shoulder of the road and studied the darkened expanse of asphalt. He could just make out the shape of a couple of bikes. What *was* the connection between the Bayou church and all those motorcycles?

He reached for the radio and gave instructions to the answering voice. "Send a deputy over to the Bayou church. Looks like we have something going on. I'm sitting on the side of the road with a civilian in the car. I'll stay where I am for the time being."

"Yes, sir," Tonya Newton, the night dispatcher, drawled. Tonya was rumor central for the sheriff's department, and without a doubt she'd be dying to know who was in his car. Too bad she wasn't going to find out.

Olivia had been alternating between studying C.J. in cop mode and keeping track of the parking lot. "I think two guys came out of the church." Her observation was punctuated by the almost deafening roar of two Harley engines.

"Yep, I'm sure they came out that door," she said with more than a bit of understatement.

"Damn," C.J. muttered. "Make sure your seat belt's tight and hang on to Fang. We may be in for a wild ride."

Two dark shapes sped off, leaving a cloud of gravel and crushed seashells in their wake.

"Tonya, they're running. I'm right on their tail. We're going south on 1518."

His voice had an edge of excitement Olivia'd never heard before. It was probably the intangible element that made him such a good law-enforcement officer.

"Turning east on Bay Road," he snapped into the radio.

The hiss and crackle of the radio were periodically interrupted by the voices of deputies racing to join the pursuit.

"Have someone check out the church," C.J. instructed Tonya, then turned to Olivia. "This doesn't feel like simple vandalism to me."

The siren was wailing as the Explorer screeched down the narrow country lane, yet C.J. could still carry on a logical conversation. Olivia liked speed, but this was ridiculous. Her fingernails were embedded in the vinyl armrest.

The radio crackled again. "Henry and Joe Don will intercept you on Farm to Market 1060." That was almost two miles up the road, and no matter how C.J. floorboarded the Explorer, the bikers were maintaining a substantial lead.

"Have Bubba get out the stop strips," he directed Tonya.

"Yes, sir. He's ready to go."

With every transmission, Tonya's voice rose an octave. Pretty soon she'd be doing a Betty Boop imitation.

"Look at that!" Olivia exclaimed.

C.J. glanced at his passenger. Her eyes were the size of dinner plates and she was pointing at the Southern Pacific locomotive racing along the adjacent train track.

"Damn!" The road would take a hard right turn across that very same track, and if the motorcycles made it they'd be long gone. If they didn't…

C.J. hit the gas, even though it was probably an exercise in futility. The train engineer obviously realized he had a *big* problem, but it was too late to stop so he laid on the horn.

Olivia closed her eyes and dug her fingernails deeper into the vinyl. If she had to meet her maker on a railroad track, she'd rather not see it coming.

The motorcycles raced across the track microseconds before the train. C.J. hit the brakes and skidded sideways, stopping so close to the track Olivia could have reached out and touched the moving train—if she'd been able to open her eyes or stop shaking or quit babbling.

"Crap! Crap! Crap!" C.J. beat on the steering wheel. "Tonya, tell me someone's on the other side of this railroad track."

There was a long hesitation before the radio responded. "No, sir. Joe Don is heading your way but he's about a half mile off."

Great! There were miles of deserted country roads and if the perps were smart enough to turn off and cut their lights, they'd never be found.

"Tonya, who responded at the church?"

The answer came back quickly. "It was Frank, and he wants to talk to you. Hang on and I'll patch him through."

C.J. tapped the steering wheel as he waited for the patch.

"Hey, boss, we've got a problem." The deputy paused as a siren sounded in the background. "The preacher's been pretty much beat to a pulp, but he ain't sayin' nuthin'. Apparently he's got himself a bad case of amnesia." The deputy snorted. "The EMT folks have just shown up. So I'll find out what they have to say."

"Okay. Tape off the area," C.J. instructed. "I'll be there in ten minutes." He turned the Explorer around and went back to town.

They drove in silence for a few minutes, then C.J. glanced at Olivia. "What the hell do you think is going on, Livy?"

Olivia gave a shrug. That was the sixty-billion-dollar question. All she knew for sure was that the place had been hoppin' ever since the Hardaways hit town.

Chapter Nineteen

Things went from bad to worse after the Bayou Church break-in. Brother Hardaway was doing a great Sergeant Schultz impression—he'd seen nothing, heard nothing and knew nothing. C.J. was surprised the dude could even put on his own socks.

And today he'd responded to a car wreck that resulted in a fistfight. Did he mention that the incident involved Mrs. Pomerantz and Gladys Schmidt? Jeez Louise. That was *all* he needed.

Paperwork was an irritation and a necessary evil, and it seemed to go on and on. C.J. was glaring at the pile of folders that had been gracing his desk for at least a week when he was distracted by the phone.

"Sheriff, the county exec is on line one."

"Put him on." C.J. stifled his impatience. "Baker here."

"Hey, Sheriff, how are things down at my cop shop?"

Not a good opening line. Jerome Bennett wasn't

known for idle chitchat, so that didn't bode well for the remainder of the conversation.

"Fine, just fine," C.J. answered, leaning back in his chair. If something was about to hit the fan, he'd rather be in a relaxed frame of mind.

"Good, good to know. I hear we had a problem out at the Bayou church last night."

"Yes, sir, we did."

There was a pause on the other end of the line. "You know we can't have people beating up our pastors. That's not seemly."

No kidding. "I've got two detectives on it. We have a description of the motorcycles." C.J. rustled some papers next to the phone. "You know what, sir? I have a call coming in on the radio that I have to take. I'll get back to you this afternoon."

No sooner had he ended the call than the phone rang again.

Now what? "Baker here."

"Well, Baker, it sounds like you could use a drink." The deep masculine voice verbalized the best idea C.J. had come across all day.

"Yeah, Delacroix, I could use a drink. How about six o'clock at the Watering Hole?"

"Done." Christian paused for a second and then said, "I have some info you're probably not going to like."

When Christian hedged like that, C.J. knew he'd flat-out hate what the man had to say.

THE WATERING HOLE WAS already bustling with the after-work crowd when C.J. arrived. Fortunately

Christian had found a booth and ordered a couple of beers and a plate of nachos.

C.J. slid into the seat across from his former partner. "What's happenin' at headquarters?" he asked. C.J. was still surprised he didn't miss his previous life in undercover narcotics.

Christian took a long draw on his beer. "Sounds like Enrique Bolivar has been tracking Selena. I think she's safe for now, but I don't know how long that'll last."

"Damn!" C.J. slammed a fist on the table, making his mug dance in place. "How did that happen? We were so careful."

"I don't think they've connected you to her, so I'm not sure how they found her. Did she do anything that would warrant publicity while she was living in Dallas?"

"I wouldn't think so. I specifically warned her about that." C.J. sighed as he sipped his beer. "What do you figure we can do?"

"Sit and wait. I'll keep my ear to the ground."

And that was all C.J. could ask. So far, his own sources had been ominously silent. He had to warn Selena, but first he wanted to see his favorite vet.

OLIVIA WAS SWAYING and gyrating to a pounding Middle Eastern beat. Belly dancing was fantastic for the glutes and abs, and what better way to feel like the Queen of Sheba. To get in the proper mood she even had her own harem outfit—midriff top, diaphanous pants, veil and finger cymbals.

Olivia was in the middle of a particularly intricate dance when the doorbell rang. "Darn!" She thought about ignoring it; however, her curiosity finally got the best of her. And when she discovered the identity of her visitor, she wished she'd followed her first instinct.

"Florene. What are you doing here?"

"Can I come in?" the preacher's wife asked, already halfway through the door.

Olivia stepped aside. It was either move or be mowed down. "Sure. Come on in."

From the minute she stepped over the sill, it was obvious Florene didn't follow the usual etiquette for houseguests. She looked more like a termite inspector than a visitor as she went from corner to corner checking everything in the living room.

What unmitigated gall! Olivia was about to complain when the brazen hussy headed into the kitchen to continue her inspection.

"Are you looking for something specific?" Olivia asked, when she could finally make her mouth move.

"Why no, hon. What makes you ask that?" Florene answered as she picked up the lid to the cookie jar.

Olivia raised an eyebrow and pointed at the lid.

"Oh, that." Florene twittered. "I guess I'm just a bit overwrought. You heard about my husband, didn't you?"

"Yes." Olivia paused for dramatic effect. "I was with the sheriff last night when he chased the guys who did it."

All the blood seemed to leave Florene's face. "Really?"

Now, that was an interesting reaction.

"Well, I'd better get going. Lots of things to do, you know." Florene scurried out of the kitchen, but prior to her exit she made time to check out the downstairs powder room.

What a nutcase. Olivia threw the dead bolt on the front door as soon as her visitor left. Then the doorbell pealed again.

Darn it! She flung open the door, ready to give Florene a piece of her mind. But whoa—it wasn't the blond bimbo.

"Hi, C.J." This was so not happening. If his lascivious grin was any indication, the guy was a huge belly-dancing fan. She clanged the finger cymbals together. "I'll get dressed."

"Oh, I think not, darlin'." He urged her into his arms. "This is a fantasy I've had since the eighth grade and I intend to savor it." And savor it he did, starting with little nibbles and kisses on her neck, down her collarbone, and across the cleavage. "Yes, ma'am, this is definitely one of my better PG-13-rated fantasies," he mumbled as he came up for air.

"But much as I'd like to continue, I came by for a reason," he said after he'd planted a long, hot kiss on her mouth. Her lack of protest appeared to be a good omen.

"I'll give you fifty cents if you'll go with me to Mom's house for dinner."

"What?"

"I'll make it a buck fifty, and throw in the fact that Mom's a great cook. Can you be ready in about thirty minutes?"

She was such a sucker for anything that man suggested. Being at his beck and call was obviously a bad plan, but for some reason she kept saying yes to his invitations. "And why do you want me to go with you? Is there something you're avoiding?"

C.J. shrugged and gave her one of his devastating little-boy looks. "Yeah, there is." He briefed her on the newest Enrique Bolivar information. "I'd love your company. Plus, you'll be a good distraction when I tell Selena her brother might be after her."

Olivia tossed her veil on the back of the couch. "Now I'm nothing but a distraction." She resisted the urge to pout.

C.J. cupped her chin and kissed her again. "Darlin' you've been a distraction to me for quite a while." He grinned just before he planted another kiss on her lips.

CORRINE WELCOMED THEM with open arms. But Selena was too busy arguing with Chandler to be very hospitable. He was sitting on one end of the sofa while she occupied the other. All they seemed to have in common was the venomous glares they exchanged. And yet the sparks flying off those two could light up half the Gulf Coast.

"How you doin'?" C.J. elbowed his brother in the side. "And how's the prettiest redhead in all of south Texas?" He walked to the end of the couch and kissed Selena's cheek. Fang followed suit and bathed her face in kisses.

"The mutt likes women, huh?" Chandler commented.

"He has good taste, just like all the Baker men." C.J. fell onto the couch between the two combatants. Fang hopped on his lap and settled down for a nap.

"Are you keeping him?" Chandler asked.

"Yep. How could I say no to Mrs. Whittaker? She taught me everything I know about fractions. Not that I ever use fractions."

Corrine put her arm around Olivia's shoulders. Like her sons, she was tall, and they were almost eye-to-eye. "I'm so glad you could come." She patted Olivia's hand. "That kid of mine never shows up for dinner. I don't know what I'm going to do with him. Come on, everyone. Supper's ready." Corrine had obviously ditched her biker-mama persona and was in full June Cleaver mode.

The aroma of roasted ham was enough to make Olivia's mouth water. "Smells wonderful, Mrs. Baker."

Corrine patted her hand again. "Call me Corrine."

Considering all the undercurrents, the meal went fairly well. Selena and Chandler were seated at opposite ends of the table, but they still managed to shoot daggers at each other. C.J., Olivia and Corrine tried valiantly to create some semblance of normalcy with their conversation, touching on a variety of topics, with more than a passing nod to small-town gossip.

"Did you hear that the Hardaways left town?" Corrine asked C.J.

He'd heard that interesting bit of news but hadn't processed exactly what it meant.

"Rumor has it that Mrs. Pomerantz was involved in a car wreck," Corrine continued. "Swear to goodness if anything happens in this town, she's right in the middle of the action."

Truer words were never spoken.

"I also heard she smacked one of the guys upside the head with her purse."

Now, why didn't that surprise him? He'd have to ask his deputy why that was omitted from the report.

"The grapevine's also reporting the guy she hit was driving a stolen car."

That much was true—the Port Serenity grapevine was better than the CIA.

The next words out of his mother's mouth made C.J. sit up and take notice.

"Apparently it was one of those rusty old Mercedes with Sonora plates."

"What?" Why hadn't someone told him that? Sonora was a state in Mexico. Mexico/Selena/Enrique—could there be a link?

Corrine paused to pass the green beans. "Yeah, Mexican plates. Since the guys involved in the wreck disappeared, Mrs. P's afraid her insurance will have to pay. More than likely it would have anyway, since she's the one who caused the accident. Potatoes?"

His mother didn't understand the bomb she'd dropped. C.J. resisted the urge to beat his head on the table. Enrique's goons must be in town. He couldn't put it off any longer—he had to warn Selena. Might as well get it over with.

"Selena honey, Christian and I just talked and the scuttlebutt he's picking up is that Enrique is trying to find you."

Every one of the freckles across her nose stood out in stark contrast to the whiteness of her skin. "Enrique? Enrique's here?" she squeaked.

C.J. went to the end of the table and put his arms around his former wife. "We don't know that for sure." He sat down in the empty chair. "Did anything happen while you were in school that got your picture in the paper? Were you involved in any kind of publicity?"

Selena chewed on her lip while she thought. "Not really."

That hesitant "not really" sent up a red flag, but C.J. remained outwardly calm. "What do you mean, *not really?*"

"You remember I did some modeling for Neiman's?"

Damn it. "Yes."

"Well, there was this write-up in the society section of the paper for one of our shows. But honestly, you couldn't tell anything from the picture."

Obviously someone could, and that was how Enrique had found her.

"Did you tell anyone you were moving down here?"

She nibbled her lip again. "Only a couple of my friends. And I had my mail forwarded to Corrine's post-office box."

He sighed. Now the question was—did they know specifically where Selena was living or were they simply trolling?

The scheme he was considering might land him in a Mexican federal prison, but if he intended to solve this problem he'd have to be proactive rather than reactive.

Chapter Twenty

Olivia'd had an early morning of surgery, and then she'd seen a never-ending stream of patients. It was definitely one of those days. Coffee—she needed coffee.

All things considered, dinner the night before had been fairly civilized. Until Corrine innocently mentioned the Mexican car, and C.J. discovered Selena's picture had been in the Dallas paper. Then everything had gone south. If some Uzi-carrying drug lord had been dogging Olivia's footsteps she wouldn't have considered posing for a newspaper picture.

One fortunate result of the dinner was that she could put any misgivings she had about C.J. and Selena to rest. Sparks between those two were nonexistent—Selena and Chandler were a completely different matter. Talk about sexual tension.

Girl talk was overdue, so Olivia picked up the phone. "Hey, Lolly, can you do lunch today?"

There was a long pause, and then a shrill screech. "You don't mind if I bring the girls, do you?" she asked.

"Nope."

"Okay. Give me an hour. Oh, darn! Gotta go." Lolly didn't give Olivia time to answer before she hung up.

Olivia stared at the receiver, grinned and hung up. Life in the mommy lane must be a challenge.

OLIVIA HEARD THE RACKET before she opened the door of the police station. The source of that noise had to be either Renee or Dana—or possibly both of the girls.

"Hey, Tiny, I can tell you've been recruited for baby-sitting duty." Olivia spoke to the harried desk sergeant. Tiny Johnson was Tonya Newton's little sister.

"Yes, ma'am." The young policewoman expertly bounced the infant into a quiet coo. "Chief had an emergency so I took—" she paused as she picked up the baby's hand to check for the nail polish "—Dana. Jimmy Bob in Homicide has Renee. Chief said to tell you she'd be finished in about fifteen minutes."

"That's okay. I'll go back and get a cup of coffee." Olivia reached out for the baby. "I'll take her so you can get back to work."

"Thanks." Tiny blew a raspberry kiss on the baby's neck before she handed her to Olivia. "Swear to goodness, those girls are cuter than a couple of speckled pups."

"They sure are," Olivia agreed as she bounced her goddaughter. She wandered through the cubicles to Homicide, lured by the sound of a deep baritone making goofy baby noises. Olivia, Lolly and Jimmy Bob had gone to high school together. Now J.B. had a whole raft of kids at home and baby talk probably qualified as a second language.

"Hey, Jimmy Bob." Olivia had played doctor with this guy when they were in kindergarten, so he'd always be Jimmy Bob to her. "I see you have the matching bookend."

He looked up and smiled. "You've got that one right, Dr. Livy. You and the chief going to lunch?"

"Uh-huh," Olivia answered, just as a pungent odor started to drift from her tiny bundle. "Are there diapers around here?"

J.B. tossed her a Huggies. "Be my guest."

"Thanks, you're a real prince."

Her snide comment elicited an even bigger chuckle.

Olivia had just secured the final piece of diaper tape when Lolly wandered into J.B.'s cubicle and collapsed into the only remaining chair.

"Lordy, Livy, I'm too old for this." Lolly slouched even lower in the chair. "We didn't get any sleep last night. When one of them went to sleep, the other one woke up." She moaned. "And now I have some bimbos selling cocaine out of their beauty shop."

"Their *beauty* shop?"

Lolly forced a grin. "Yeah, the Cutie Curl out on the highway. Only in south Texas can a girl get a perm and snort a line at the same time."

Lolly took the baby from J.B. "Thanks a million." She turned to Olivia. "Let's get out of here while the gettin's good. The stroller is by the back door. If we're really quiet we can sneak out before anyone else stops me."

ALTHOUGH THEY'D MISSED the lunch-hour rush, Daisy's Diner was still crowded. Miraculously, the twins were both asleep in their stroller. Lolly sighed and ordered a glass of iced tea.

"This is *so* hard." She was referring to being a full-time mom and a part-time police chief. "I don't know how I'll manage when I have to go back to work full days."

"When do you plan to do that?"

"In a couple of months. Mee Maw will babysit until I can find a nanny. One week she and Aunt Sissy are talking about opening a boutique, and the next week they're planning a road trip. From the snippets of conversation I've been hearing, my 'uh-oh' meter is twitching like a frog in a pot of boiling water." Lolly grinned as she picked up the menu. "So I really do have to get a good sitter. Please, let me find one who doesn't have a rap sheet and likes to bake chocolate chip cookies."

The waitress arrived to take their order. "I'll have the chicken salad and another iced tea," Olivia said.

Lolly nibbled on her lower lip. "I've lost almost all my baby weight and I'm dying for something fattening." She looked up at the waitress. "Cheeseburger, fries and a chocolate milkshake." She waited until the waitress left.

"Okay, give."

Nothing got by that sharp-eyed cop. "Hmm." Olivia stalled. "Well… It's C.J."

"Well, duh," Lolly murmured.

"Yeah, well, hmm, I have a bit of a problem." She

filled Lolly in on her errant love life and the man who was playing a starring role. "I finally came to the realization that he and Selena are just friends."

Lolly's look was as eloquent as the unspoken "no kidding."

"Yeah, okay. I'm a doofus."

Lolly raised an eyebrow.

"So the question is—what do I do now? I still have this little issue with trust." Olivia wanted to wail but she managed to control herself. She had to be careful because the rumor mill had spies everywhere. And unlike Las Vegas, what was said at Daisy's didn't always stay at Daisy's.

"A *little* issue?"

"Okay, smarty, I have a huge issue with trust." There was a lull in the conversation when the waitress brought their food. Olivia compared her plate of salad to Lolly's juicy burger and wished she'd splurged. Sometimes a girl needed an artery-clogging treat. She snatched a fry off her friend's plate.

"I suppose I should admit it. I'm in love with the guy," Olivia said and wished the iced tea would magically turn into a Cuervo Golden Margarita.

"Yeah."

"But what do I do? I've really messed things up."

"Is he still asking you out?"

"Yeah." It was Olivia's turn for monosyllabic answers.

"Is he still being attentive?"

"Yeah."

"Have you seen him out with anyone else?"

"No."

"I rest my case. You need to stop worrying and let things run their natural course."

Her friend was right, but patience was not Olivia's strong suit.

Chapter Twenty-One

Several days had passed since Olivia's C.J. epiphany. Darn it—now that she'd uttered the *L* word the guy had disappeared off the radar screen. Poof, vanished, dis-ap-peared. So when Mama offered chicken and dumplings for dinner, Olivia immediately accepted the invitation.

Rose locked the door of her gallery and jumped into Olivia's 'Vette. "Would you take me out to the Super Saver before we go home? I need to pick up some motor oil for your daddy. I was supposed to do it days ago, but I keep forgetting."

The Super Saver parking lot was in typical jam-and-cram mode, but after driving around they found a place near the Dumpster. A Dumpster next to her beloved car—yikes! Olivia resisted the urge to pat the fender as she reluctantly followed Rose into the store.

Mama marched off to the auto section. She was obviously a woman on a mission. Olivia wandered through the shampoo aisle, perused greeting cards and was engrossed in a selection of new books when a hard object was poked against the center of her back. Olivia's first reaction was to yell at the idiot, and her second was to faint dead away. Because as sure as God made little green apples, it was a gun.

"What do you want?" she squeaked. Good Lord—people didn't get kidnapped at the Super Saver.

"Just shut up and walk to the front door." The gravelly voice had a faint accent she couldn't quite place.

"What do you want?" she whispered a second time but kept moving. All she could see of her assailant was the tail of his bright red shirt.

"Shut up!" He poked her again. "You got something we want, and you're gonna give it to us or you'll be sorry." He emphasized his demand with another thrust of the gun.

Well, he darned sure didn't mean money. Every spare cent Olivia had went to student loans and house payments. "If it's money you want—"

Olivia didn't get a chance to finish her sentence before the jerk slapped a hand over her mouth and hauled her into a rack of cut-price jeans.

"I ain't kidding. Where is it?" The idiot was built like a steamroller, smelled like a cesspool and had a skull and crossbones tattooed on his hand. This dude was *not* a member of the Chamber of Commerce.

"What are you doing to my daughter?" Rose shrieked, providing Olivia with the distraction she needed to grab his "package" and squeeze with all her might. The guy dropped to his knees, keening like a banshee.

"Run!" Olivia grabbed Rose's hand and sprinted toward the front door. She wasn't sure the security folks at the Super Saver were ready for this bad guy. They'd almost made it through the electronic-eye door when sanity prevailed. Olivia slid to a halt so fast her mother skidded into her. "What am I thinking?" She slapped a palm to her head. "We need to find out what he wanted."

Olivia raced back to the book section, but although the man had been wailing in agony when last seen, he had since managed to disappear. "We *have* to find him. You take that aisle. I'll take this one," Olivia instructed as she ran from row to row in a futile search. She punched in C.J.'s number on her cell phone, but before it connected she spotted her prey shuffling out the front door.

"Mom, Mom," she shouted and heads turned all over the store. With luck, security wouldn't get their act together and arrest the two of them.

Rose rounded the corner clutching her heart. "Lord in heaven, child. You almost gave me a heart attack."

"He's leaving. Let's go!" That was all it took for Rose to join Olivia in a sprint out of the store.

"Damn! I knew we shouldn't have parked by the Dumpster," Olivia exclaimed. They were running to the 'Vette when a huge black-and-chrome Harley sped off.

"There he is!" Olivia recognized the shirt. Realizing her chance to catch the guy was less than nil, Olivia called in the cavalry—Sheriff C. J. Baker.

With one hand on the wheel and the other on her cell phone, Olivia peeled out of the lot and headed for the highway.

"There he is!" Rose yelled and Olivia responded by laying rubber. The last thing Olivia heard before she threw the phone on the console was a muffled, "Don't you dare chase him."

Sure thing.

Unfortunately, the Harley had a three-block start and by the time Olivia and Rose reached the boulevard where they'd spotted him the guy had disappeared. Vanished. Not surprising, since there were any number of fast-food joints, tourist traps and strip malls he could've pulled behind to hide.

"Damn!"

"Yeah, double damn! What did C.J. say?"

"He said not to chase him." Olivia arched an eyebrow. "Like I'd let the idiot get away if I can help it." Their search was fruitless and now they were in the Kentucky Fried Chicken parking lot checking out cars.

"Is he sending someone?"

"Yep. I think I hear a siren. C.J. isn't going to be happy with me. He told me not to give chase and I ignored him."

"Uh-huh." Rose concurred. "That was probably stupid. The guy had a gun."

"Mother, please! He also has a debilitating injury." Olivia giggled at the thought.

Rose's chuckle was interrupted by the piercing scream of a siren. "Here come the cops. Let's give them a quick statement and get out of here."

That sounded like a great idea. She already knew C.J. wasn't going to be sympathetic and he probably wasn't more than five minutes behind the first responder.

The deputy drove up, cut the siren and ambled over. "Are you ladies okay?"

"Yes, we are," Olivia assured him. Then she gave him a description of the man and the bike. "Do you think we could go home now? My mother isn't feeling well."

Rose bolstered the fib by doing a great wilting violet routine.

"Well, I don't know, ma'am. I'm not sure the sheriff's gonna be too happy with that." The young deputy rolled back on his heels, obviously contemplating the situation.

Rose doubled over and moaned.

"Please, my mom has to have her medicine. If the sheriff needs us, he has my phone number." Olivia pulled out all the stops on her southern belle routine.

And what red-blooded American male could resist that? "Okay, you ladies drive real careful going home." He leaned in and spoke to Rose. "Miz Alvarado, you take good care of yourself now. You hear?"

Olivia maintained her stoic look until they were out of sight, then she lost it. "Mama, swear to goodness you're the best."

"I know." Rose puffed up with pride. "Let's go home. A big plate of dumplings will make us feel better."

Olivia could only agree.

Chapter Twenty-Two

Olivia was digging into her second plate of chicken when C.J. barged into the Alvarados' kitchen without bothering to knock.

He sat right down and grabbed the fork from her hand. "I thought I told you not to chase that man!" He stabbed the utensil into a steaming dumpling. "You could've gotten killed!" C.J. punctuated his remarks by shoving the morsel into his mouth and chewing furiously.

"Nice to see you, C.J.," Rose said with just a bit of irony. "Would you like a plate of your own?"

It finally dawned on him what he'd done, and his good manners kicked in. "Yes, ma'am. That'd be real nice." C.J. stood and offered his hand to Olivia's dad. "Raul, how you doin'?" he asked.

"Not too bad. I'd be doing better if these two could stay out of trouble." He indicated his wife and daughter. "Their shenanigans are enough to make a guy go gray."

Wasn't that the truth. C.J. sat down again and before he knew it he had his own plate piled high with food.

"Can you cook like this?" he asked Olivia. She shot him a venomous glare. Nothing like living dangerously to spur a man's appetite.

Eventually C.J. folded his napkin and leaned back in the chair. "What do you think went down at the Super Saver?"

Rose and Olivia started talking at the same time, each of them providing an opinion.

His gut told him he had big problems in his county, and it was the same intuition that had already kept him alive more times than he wanted to count. He was pretty sure the guys in the Mercedes had some connection with Selena. But what was going on with Olivia? He suspected it involved the Hardaways, but he'd run into a brick wall talking to those folks. And now they'd disappeared.

C.J. retrieved a small notebook from his pocket. "Tell me exactly what he said."

Olivia wrinkled her nose. "Let me see." She paused, trying to remember the exact words. "He said I had something he wanted."

Okay, that was new. "What do you think he meant?"

"Beats me." She looked at Rose for advice. "Mama, can you think of anything?"

"I've racked my brain since we got back from the Super Saver, but I can't come up with a thing," Rose said.

"Seen or heard anything unusual lately?"

"Not that I remember." Olivia had a feeling there was *something* but she couldn't come up with it.

"Mrs. Alvarado, how about you?"

"No, nothing."

Olivia nodded, then broke the grim atmosphere by laughing. "You should've seen that guy when I got through with him. He'll be singing soprano for at least a month."

Just the thought! C.J. resisted the urge to cringe. "Remind me to never cross these women, would you please?" he implored Raul.

"That's always a good idea," Raul concurred, flinching when his wife hit him on the arm.

"I think you should stay with your parents until we discover what's happening." C.J. made the suggestion, even though he knew Olivia wouldn't agree.

"Are you kidding? I'm going home."

Uh-oh—she had on her stubborn face. He noticed that Raul and Rose didn't bother to comment; they *had* lived with her for years, after all.

"Okay." He rubbed his chin, contemplating his next move. "I'll follow you home and check out the house."

"That's a wonderful idea," Rose said before Olivia could respond. She went to the cabinet, pulled out two tinfoil pans and filled them with leftovers. "Why don't you do that right now?" She shoved the pans into C.J.'s hands.

"Mother!"

Mama was matchmaking again.

"Shoo." Rose made a flapping motion with her hands. "I'm about to get a headache."

Raul made a muffled noise that sounded suspiciously like an abbreviated laugh and Fang barked in delight.

THE SEARCH OF Olivia's house revealed nothing more sinister than dust bunnies. Fang made another circle of the kitchen island looking for stray morsels.

"I can't believe my parents." Olivia joined him in the kitchen. She felt compelled to gripe, even though she really *was* glad C.J. was there. "Is it all clear?"

"Yep. Not a bad guy in sight." He slid the leftovers into the refrigerator, then quietly walked to the island and cupped her chin. "Seriously, I think you'd be better off at your parents' house. At least it would make me feel better."

"Yeah, well, I know what would make *me* feel better." After a hard-fought internal struggle Olivia had finally accepted that she loved this man, and more importantly, trusted him. She was finally over the Brian debacle—and that felt great. It was time to fess up that she'd made a terrible mistake by leaving C.J.'s house in the middle of the night.

Olivia put her arms around his neck, pausing a moment to savor the stubble on his cheeks, and then threaded her fingers through his silky hair. This had been a particularly favorite daydream. "We have some unfinished business, cowboy." She barely had time to verbalize the thought when he brought his lips to hers and she went into a major meltdown. He'd obviously been waiting for this, too. And it felt oh, so much like coming home.

The country-western song about the man with the slow hands fit C.J. to a tee. He touched and caressed every square inch of her skin as he unveiled it. Olivia was almost delirious by the time he got to the really good parts, and from the gleam in his eye, she could tell he knew exactly what he was doing. But that was okay; her turn was coming.

It wasn't fair. Somehow he'd managed to get her stripped down to a pair of lacy bikinis and her sandals, but he still had on the faded jeans she loved so much, and the chambray shirt that made her think of Butch Cassidy and the Sundance Kid. He was nibbling on her neck, an activity that never failed to give her goose bumps. Hmm—darn his hide. He knew she couldn't resist *that*. Not that she had intended to resist *anything*. "You have way too many clothes on," she murmured, drawing him toward the bedroom as Fang danced around their feet.

"No way," he muttered as he pinned her against the wall and proceeded to kiss and nibble and suck every square inch of her body. When he was finished, he started all over again. That man sure had a way about him. Which was the last cogent thought Olivia had.

SOMEHOW THEY MADE IT to the bed, where they ended up in a tangle of arms and legs. Olivia was lying halfway on top of him, running her fingers through the thick hair on his chest. Although he was blond, the hair on his chest was dark brown.

"Do you dye your hair?" she asked with a smirk, knowing the question would get a rise out of him. And she wasn't wrong.

He jerked up. "What!"

"Your hair's blond and this—" she tweaked it "—is brown."

"Ouch." He grabbed her hand. "That hurts. But I know what you're up to, so you'd better watch out." With that proclamation, he pulled her down for another soul-searing kiss, and a *whole* lot of other yummy things.

OLIVIA'S LIFE HAD BEEN CRAZY. First there'd been the Peeping Tom incident, and then the Super Saver situation. Thank goodness she had the sexiest lawman south of the Red River in her corner. He was sweet and protective, and behind the cocky, bad-boy grin lurked a steely-eyed cop with a soft heart. That was a potent and formidable combo.

It felt good to trust again. And to be perfectly honest the transformation had started the first time he'd planted those wonderfully warm lips on hers. No doubt about it, she was toast. All golden-brown and buttered!

Chapter Twenty-Three

"Get up, sleepyhead. Fang wants to talk to you."

Olivia tried to ignore C.J.'s voice as she burrowed into the pillow. She couldn't ignore the cold wet nose and puppy kisses, however. She was so, so tired—not surprising considering how they'd spent the night and a nap sounded so, so good.

"Wakey, wakey, tea and cakey."

"Go away," she muttered, but when she cracked an eye C.J. was at the foot of her bed holding a white paper bag. Breakfast tacos. Just the smell made her ravenous. How did he know that egg-and-chorizo breakfast tacos were her all-time favorite?

"Do you have Tater Tots in there, too?" she asked. He held up another sack, this one from the Tastee Treat. Grease was already seeping through the brown paper. Nothing like junk food to jump-start the day.

Olivia grinned and jerked down the sheet, exposing most of her assets. "Why don't you sit down and join me?"

He grinned and those irresistible dimples made an

appearance. "Yes, ma'am, thought you'd never ask." He dropped the bags on the bed and got out of his clothes. The tacos would have to wait.

SEVERAL HOURS AND a communal shower later—and who would forget that trick he did with the soap?— he offered a suggestion for the rest of the weekend.

"I called my lieutenant and told him I'm taking a couple of personal days. Fang has an invitation to go to Grandma Corrine's house, so let's visit San Antonio for the weekend," he said.

Fortunately she wasn't on call. "What do you want to do?" Olivia had visions of dinner on the River Walk and a romantic stroll along the lazy San Antonio River.

"It's a surprise," C.J. said with a sexy wink. Her fantasy was almost a fait accompli.

THE FLAT-AS-A-TABLETOP coastal terrain soon gave way to miles and miles of undulating grassland. Live oaks, mesquite thickets and herds of grazing cattle provided the only visual landmarks in the land between the Gulf Coast and San Antonio.

C.J. broke into Olivia's hypnotic trance. "Do you want to stop at Three Rivers for one of those famous Dairy Queen milkshakes?" he drawled. Christian had proposed to Lolly by slipping a ring into a milkshake at that very same Dairy Queen.

The idea warranted a big smile. "Sure. But I think I'll have a Butterfinger Blizzard."

"You got it." He signaled for an exit off the freeway and turned toward the small town and nirvana.

"Hmm. That was good." Olivia rubbed her stomach.

"Do you want another one?"

"Are you kidding? That was probably worth two pounds right here." She patted her hip as picked up her purse. "I have to hit the ladies' room. Once we get on the freeway, there's nothing for miles except sagebrush and mesquite trees." And the last time she'd peed in a field she'd ended up with a bad case of poison ivy.

When they arrived in San Antonio, C.J. passed the exit to the downtown and River Walk, skirted the loop road leading to the area's glitziest shopping center and sailed past all the best restaurants.

"Okay, I give up. Where *are* we going?" she asked. Her fantasy had involved at least one night at La Mansion, one of the most romantic hotels on the river. But unfortunately, they weren't anywhere *near* the river.

"Fiesta Texas," he answered as he pulled into the parking lot of the theme park.

"Are you kidding me?" she shrieked excitedly. She was a roller-coaster junkie and Fiesta Texas was one of her favorite places.

The skies were sapphire-blue and the May heat was already scorching. C.J. handed her a baseball cap, which she set firmly on her head, pulling her ponytail out the back opening.

"See why I told you to wear shorts?" They strolled to the main entrance, amid a bevy of families with kids.

Built on the remains of an old rock quarry in the rolling terrain of the Texas Hill Country, Fiesta Texas provided all the adrenaline, junk food and frenetic energy that any kid, or kid at heart, could want from a one-day pass.

The park mirrored the paisley print of cultural heritage indigenous to San Antonio. Rides had names like the Rattler, Der Rollschuhcoaster, the Gully Washer and the Rodeo Rider.

"First things first," Olivia announced when they strolled into the park. "I want to go to Billy Bob's River Café for barbecue."

Sounded like a plan to him. C.J. never turned down a good meal. So they pigged out on succulent brisket, potato salad, coleslaw and peach cobbler.

"You ready to hit the rides?" he asked.

"Absolutely," she called over her shoulder as she flitted off to the Rattler, one of the country's largest wooden roller-coasters.

Lolly had tried it once and then absolutely refused to go again. She'd freaked when the cars flew into the abyss of the quarry canyon, screeched to the top of the cliff and disappeared into a tunnel in the cliff wall.

But C.J. was also an adrenaline junkie and pronounced the ride a pure rush. A couple of kids seated behind them screamed the entire time, but when the train slid into the station Olivia heard them say they were going again. Lordy mercy! If she lived to be a thousand, she'd never understand the mind of the munchkin.

From there the couple went to the Scream, a 200-foot skyrocketing free fall that left Olivia breathless. After that it was on to the Poltergeist. Talk about an appropriate name—this one launched its rider from zero to sixty miles an hour in 3.5 seconds. Now if that didn't scare the heck out of you, nothing would.

"How about the Gully Washer," C.J. suggested next.

It was hot as Hades, but then, this *was* South Texas and heat was par for the course. However, a drenching sounded wonderful. "Okay, let's go."

When they finished with the white-water rapids they were soaking wet and it felt delicious. And speaking of wet T-shirts—the teenage attendant who spied Olivia about went into apoplexy. C.J. couldn't blame him. No, siree!

"Are you ready to sit under a tree and rest for a few minutes?" C.J. asked.

She nodded happily.

"Wait there and I'll go find us something to drink." He indicated an empty bench under the shade of a massive live oak.

Olivia leaned her head back and enjoyed the cool breeze. Hmm—this felt *so* good. She was contemplating a nap when C.J. returned with two cups of icy lemonade. He could've offered her the crown jewels and they wouldn't have been more appealing.

"Here you go. Hope this is okay."

"Oh, yeah. I feel like I've been laid out on a griddle to brown," Olivia said as she gulped down her drink.

IN AN EFFORT to get a breeze Olivia fanned the front of her T-shirt. Damn—that woman could make scrubbing floors look sexy and the T-shirt, well… He grabbed her hand in mid-flap.

"I've been thinking about this for a while. I realize you're supposed to have champagne and roses, but this seems more appropriate." C.J. fingered the huge plastic Cracker Jack ring he had in his pocket.

It would either be the best day of his life or the worst. If she refused, it would definitely be the worst. He took the gaudy ring from his pocket and put it on the third finger of her left hand. "I love you and I want to marry you." There, he'd said it—for better or worse. And he sure hoped it was for better.

Her belly laugh was probably not a good sign. Then she slapped a hand over her mouth and made a strangling noise. Every time she looked at her hand, she broke into gales of laugher.

Well, damn. This *was* going to be the day from hell.

When she could finally control her giggles, she said, "You're kidding, right?"

Obviously the Cracker Jack ring was a strategic error. "No, I wasn't kidding. The ring is a joke, but if you say yes I'll buy you any ring you want."

She held up her hand and gaped.

It was time for him to take some decisive action. "Come here." C.J. pulled her into his arms and stroked her back. Tears dampened his shirt. Maybe they were tears of happiness, but hey, he was just a guy and guys were notoriously bad at deciphering the female mind. Deciding in for a penny and all that rot, he forged ahead. "All you have to do is say yes."

His comment was greeted by another strangled noise. Jeez, he should probably ditch the optimism.

He raised her chin and kissed her. "Do you love me?"

Olivia nodded.

"Will you marry me?"

She nodded again.

Praise the Lord and pass the ammunition!

Olivia gazed at the awful plastic ring. Even though he'd made vague noises about the future, she'd expected to have plenty of time to make a logical decision. But no—the dope had sprung it on her right in front of Bugs Bunny. For that reason, if no other, she should politely decline.

No way. He might be a dope, but he was her dope.

C.J. jumped up and pulled Olivia with him. "We're off to North Star mall."

Olivia wasn't thinking about his promise to buy her any ring she wanted. "I'm hot and sticky and my nose is sunburned. Why would I want to go shopping at North Star Mall?" She referred to the most glamorous shopping center in San Antonio.

The grin he produced was heart stopping. He picked up her hand and kissed the palm. "Darlin', we're gonna buy us a ring."

And who could argue with that?

"And after we buy this ring, are you up for a weekend at La Mansion?"

"Oh, yes, sir. That's the best idea I've ever heard."

Chapter Twenty-Four

Selena was bored. C.J. was away for the weekend, Corrine was out with biker Dan, and Fang was napping. Plus, she was about to break out in hives from being around Chandler Baker 24/7. He was rude to the point of being obnoxious and had on numerous occasions rebuffed her offers to help with his physical therapy. Oooh, no—the idiot would rather drive to Corpus Christi every day than accept help from *her*.

But it was probably for the best. She wouldn't consider putting her hands on that man. She sighed. Who did she think she was kidding?

Aargh! She had to get out of the house but C.J. had threatened to lock her in her room if she as much as considered going to town. Even a trip to Piggly Wiggly was sounding like a great outing—and the mere thought of Dillard's department store sent her heart into palpitations. It was broad daylight, for goodness sake. What could happen at Piggly Wiggly?

Considering her luck, probably a lot, but she was going to the grocery store, anyway.

Why did she always feel compelled to tempt fate? Why? Why? Why?

As SELENA WAS LOADING the groceries in the back of Corrine's car, she felt, rather than heard someone walk up. Before she could react, a strong hand covered her mouth and lifted her off her feet.

Big, big uh-oh! A rusted Mercedes drove up and the driver opened the trunk. Before she knew what had happened, she was unceremoniously dumped inside. *Madre de Dios!*

Don't panic. Don't panic. Don't panic. Selena felt faint. Deep breath. Deep breath. Keep breathing. Breathing's good. Remember the survival course from freshman year and whatever you do, don't hyperventilate. She could hear a muffled horn. She hoped someone had seen what happened, but she didn't have the luxury of waiting to be rescued. If these jerks worked for Enrique, all bets were off.

It was hotter than hell in the car trunk and sweat was dripping from every pore. Even her hands were slick. What had the instructor of that course said about the panels on the taillights? All she could remember was his fine tight buns. Get a grip, girl, and think! Think. Think. Think.

Then she remembered—pop the cover off the taillights so she could see. Then there was something about a trunk release latch. *That's right.* The guy said to look for the doohickey under the carpet. Please

God, let this piece of dog doo have a doohickey under the carpet.

She broke several nails trying to rip up the trunk liner. Piggly Wiggly was in the middle of town, so that gave her a few minutes' grace. If she knew Enrique, and she knew Enrique better than she wanted to, they were on their way to the marina to smuggle her back to South America. And South America was the last place she planned to go.

The carpet gave way with a snap and Selena whacked her head so hard she saw stars. Then she realized in all the time they'd been driving they'd never come to a full stop. That meant the idiots were running stop signs and red lights—and wasn't it a good thing that brains weren't a requisite for Enrique's employees? What was with all that horn honking?

Holy mother—there was a latch. She said a half-dozen Hail Marys and pulled as hard as she could. The trunk lid rose almost an inch and through the opening she could see a white minivan right on their bumper. Thank goodness, someone in the van was honking the horn.

While she scrambled to find a makeshift tool to pry the trunk all the way open, the minivan slid into the lane next to the Mercedes. The next thing Selena knew, there was a crunch on the driver's side. The minivan was trying to force them off the road. Thank you, God!

As if under the influence of divine intervention, her hand touched cold steel in the form of a crowbar.

Another crunch of metal on metal and she had the

trunk open. The Mercedes had skidded to a stop and was resting against a telephone pole, so Selena wasted no time in jumping out. She looked over her shoulder and saw that her abductors were temporarily out of commission. The door to the van slid open and a feminine voice screamed at her to get in.

She didn't need a second invitation. Her savior was Lorraine Hightower, an English teacher at the high school—short, plump, overpermed and obviously a NASCAR wannabe. Thank you, God.

"You want to go to the city cops or the county mounties?" She executed an expert spin and hit the gas.

"County, definitely the sheriff's office." Selena took a deep breath. Swear to God she'd never fantasize about a produce section again.

Chapter Twenty-Five

The minute C.J. returned from his weekend in San Antonio he was hit with the news of Selena's abduction. Damnation. It had to be Enrique.

C.J. and his deputies watched the Piggly Wiggly security tape over, and over, and over.

"Damn it! Why are these tapes so bad?" he exclaimed. The actual kidnapping was grainy but the crime was obvious; the license plate and any other identifying marks on the Mercedes were not. It probably didn't matter. The plates on the Mercedes involved in the wreck with Mrs. Pomerantz had been stolen.

"Darn good thing Miz Hightower had to get her high blood pressure prescription refilled." Although the comment came from one of the deputies, it echoed C.J.'s thoughts exactly. No telling what would have happened if Mrs. Hightower hadn't been there. However, Selena wasn't any slouch in the survival department. C.J. was proud of her.

"Any hits on the car?" he asked even though he knew the deputies would alert him the minute anything turned up. When the police had arrived at the scene, the Mercedes was long gone. The only thing left was a hubcap and a smear of paint. Not much to go on.

"Nope, boss. My guess is that they're holed up in some dive in Corpus Christi." That came from C.J.'s second-in-command. "And they probably took the car to a wrecking yard. We have the Corpus cops looking for a junker Mercedes with a smashed-in side."

"Good." He dismissed the deputies and put his booted feet on the desk. It was his favorite position for meditating.

He'd thrown the entire resources of his department into finding the scumbags who'd assaulted Olivia and tried to kidnap Selena. He was sure he was after two different perps, and they'd both managed to simply vanish.

Could Olivia and Selena be involved in a random crime wave? Not likely. He was ninety-nine percent sure Enrique was the threat to Selena; as for Olivia's assailant, he didn't have a clue. So he figured he'd start with the enemy he knew. C.J. pulled his feet off the desk and picked up the phone. This outlandish idea had been brewing for a while—and now was the time to put it into action.

THEY AGREED TO MEET at the Watering Hole, because it was the only place Fang would be welcome and it was too hot for him to wait in the car. C.J. was already in their favorite booth when Christian arrived.

"Hey, partner, what's up?" Christian greeted his friend and reached down to scratch behind Fang's ears.

"You want the good news first?" C.J. asked as his friend settled in the booth.

"Sure."

"I gave Livy a ring yesterday."

"Hot damn! Congratulations."

"Thanks. I'm a happy man."

"When's the big day?"

"Don't know. We haven't gotten that far."

Christian called a waitress over and ordered. "So hit me with the bad news."

C.J. ran a finger over the condensation on his glass of iced tea before he answered. "Selena was kidnapped and thrown in the trunk of a car in the middle of the Piggly Wiggly parking lot."

"Really! She okay?" Christian asked.

"Yeah. She took a course on survival skills in college. Apparently they taught them how to get out of a car trunk. And Mrs. Hightower from the high school rode to the rescue, so Selena is okay. Scared, but okay."

"Enrique?"

"Yeah, I'm pretty certain his goons were the culprits. But I have to make sure I'm right. If he's the guy, I have an idea." C.J. took a big swallow of tea. "We've got to get rid of Enrique once and for all, and I need your help. But feel free at any time to tell me to take a hike. This one is really off the wall."

Christian grinned, but his smile fell short of being humorous. "You know I like off the wall. Tell me."

When C.J. finished outlining his idea, Christian whooped. "Man! You're the most devious son-of-a-gun I've ever met, ya know that?"

Yeah, C.J. was aware of that fact. "Do you think it'll work?"

"As a matter of fact, I think it will. We'd better not get caught, though, because sure as shootin' they'd throw our butts under their jail."

Ain't that the truth!

Chapter Twenty-Six

Selena had promised C.J. that she'd stay home. Logic told her he was right.

But the more she thought about it, the more determined she was to take control of her life. And if that control meant a 9mm Glock, so be it. Damn Enrique, anyway. She'd taken the survival course as a lark, but thank God she'd taken it. Who would *really* expect to be thrown into the trunk of a car?

The next time brother dearest or any of his stupid goons tried something, Selena planned to be prepared. It had been quite a test of her devious skills to sneak away successfully from Corrine and Chandler, but the mission had been accomplished. Bureaucratic hoops were a nightmare; however, Selena was now the proud owner of her very own Dirty Harry. Firearms training had been another course she'd taken. So come and get it, Enrique, because this girl wasn't going down without a fight.

Now that Selena's primary mission had been accomplished, it was time for a little retail therapy—

possibly a new pair of sandals, a sexy little sundress or some new makeup. Where was the nearest Bobbie Brooks counter?

The last swipe of mascara was barely dry when her good mood was interrupted by an obnoxious male voice. Chandler—sexy, insufferable Chandler. Why was it that C.J. was the only male in her life worth a peso?

"What the hell do you think you're doing?" he snarled.

Selena swirled on her stool, oblivious to the admiring looks Chandler was getting from the makeup artist. "Hello, Chandler, nice to see you, too." She'd be damned if she'd let him make her mad.

"Let's get out of here." He made a grab for her hand, but missed. Just the thought of her prancing around a mall with Enrique's goons on the loose made his blood boil.

Selena ignored him as she tipped the blonde with the mascara wand. "Thanks for the compliment, Chandler. I like my new look, too." She picked up her shopping bags and deliberately sashayed away. Unfortunately, her cold shoulder didn't deter him for long.

"Don't you realize someone is trying to kidnap you?" He was louder than he'd intended to be, and lowered his voice for the next accusation. "Do you have a brain in that pretty little head of yours?" He emphasized the insult by grabbing her arm.

Enough was enough. "Yes, I know that. I do have a brain, and I don't give a damn what you think," she muttered, getting right into his face. "And secondly,

I don't have any desire to become acquainted with the security folks in this department store. So if you want to talk and you think you can keep it civil, I'll let you buy me a cup of coffee." She marched out the door leading to the mall. Chandler complained all the way to the coffee shop.

"Okay." He rubbed his face as he took a sip of coffee. "Let me start over. I couldn't believe it when I discovered you were gone. On a hunch, I decided to try the mall. I'm worried about you. Enrique is dangerous."

He was speaking to her as if she was a particularly slow learner. The man actually cared! That realization almost modified her response, but not quite.

"You know what, Chandler? Nothing irritates me faster than a condescending jerk. Of course I know I'm in danger. But I'll go straight over the edge if I'm stuck in the house much longer. So I'm doing some shopping. It makes me feel better." That wasn't exactly a truthful answer, but he didn't need to know she had a gun. She took a decisive bite of her cheese Danish.

Chandler massaged the bridge of his nose, then picked up her hand. "I realize I've been hard to live with, and I'll also admit I'm a card-carrying knuckle-head. But I have a proposition." He held her hand between both of his. "Let's start over."

Lulled by the conciliatory tone of his voice, and the fact she was sick of being on edge, Selena reluctantly agreed. When sleep eluded her in the dead of night she would sometimes admit that a great deal of the tension with Chandler, at least on her part, was sexual in origin—not that she had a chance in the world of its being reciprocated. Way to go, girl! So if he was willing to call a truce, it was okay with her.

"How about we get some lunch, and then I'll follow you home."

The perverse idea of testing his new tolerance took root. "I'm not through shopping."

Chandler looked like he wanted to bolt, but he held firm. "I'll go with you."

"Are you sure?" Selena smiled sweetly.

"Yeah, I'm positive." He seemed anything but enthusiastic.

"Great, let's go to Victoria's Secret."

This time he truly did look as if he had just crunched a cockroach.

C.J. HAD HIS HEAD POKED INTO the Baker family refrigerator studying his snack choices when Chandler swatted his butt. In a repeat of an oft-played scene from their childhood, C.J. jerked up and clobbered his noggin. Fang scampered around their feet, sure this was some kind of fun game.

"Hey, dimwit. I could get a concussion." C.J. rubbed the top of his head.

"Not with a head that hard, you couldn't."

C.J. let that one slide. "We need to talk." He took two Cokes out of the refrigerator and tossed one to Chandler.

"Where's Mom?"

Chandler sat down and popped the lid of his soft drink. "She's out somewhere with Dan the Man."

Both men shuddered at the thought of A) their mother having a boyfriend, and B) their mother being a Harley babe.

"Have you seen her all duded up in her leathers?" Chandler asked.

C.J. thankfully could say he'd missed that pleasure. What was the world coming to? Mothers in leather. "Nope, can't say I have."

"Well, let me tell you. She's something else."

Too much information. "Where's Selena?"

"She's camped out in her room. Do you realize she went to the mall in Corpus this morning?" Chandler paused. "I about had a heart attack when I found her."

"Good Lord! What is *wrong* with that girl?"

"I don't know what she was thinking." Chandler shook his head. "But we have to do something about this Enrique situation, quick."

It was the first time C.J. had ever heard Chandler express an interest in Selena's problems. That was good for two reasons. First of all, C.J. suspected his brother had strong feelings for Selena that he was denying, and secondly, his help was essential in pulling off C.J.'s scheme without anyone getting arrested or killed. Fortunately, Chandler's therapy had worked and he was back in fighting form.

"I have an idea." He filled Chandler in on the general concept of his plan.

After he'd finished, Chandler set his Coke on the table. "God, you're unbelievable." He shook his head. "But it might work. It just might work. When do we begin?"

"As soon as possible," C.J. answered. "But first we have to have a family confab." As much as he wanted to help Selena, and he truly did want to keep her safe, he also wanted to tell his family about his engagement. Corrine would be ecstatic; Selena was going to be mildly surprised but happy for him, and Chandler would hoist a beer in honor of the occasion.

THROUGH CHRISTIAN'S South American contacts, they'd determined that there was a bounty on Selena's head. Good old Enrique, the scum-sucking pig, had bartered his sister to a pervert named Hector Solis for a bigger cut of the Miami drug trade. C.J. remembered Hector—he had already buried three younger wives, and Selena was not about to become his fourth.

C.J., Chandler and Christian were scheduled to meet at the Shrimp Shack, a typical Gulf Coast fast-food joint where everything except the coleslaw was cooked in the same grease—shrimp, fish, chicken, even the fries. A family with a passel of towheaded children abandoned the booth by the kitchen, leaving a trail of crumbs, ketchup smears and all the other flotsam and jetsam associated with kid dining.

C.J. had ordered a Lone Star and was halfway through the beer when Christian joined him, followed shortly by Chandler.

"I ordered three baskets of shrimp. Hope that's okay," he informed his companions.

"Sure. Did you order me a beer?" Christian asked, and when C.J. shook his head he hailed the waitress.

The waitress returned shortly with their drinks, and after she left, they began their strategy session.

"I've sketched out the entire operation. If you think it's stupid as all hell, let me know now," C.J. said.

When he finished, the silence at the table was complete. Christian and Chandler were either overwhelmed at his audacity or astonished at his stupidity. He hoped it was the former.

Chandler finally broke the silence. "I'm sure I know the answer, but I have to ask. Are you guys sure you have the contacts you need to pull this off?"

C.J. glanced at his former partner. "With Christian's help, we do. And I know a couple of deep-cover DEA guys who owe me big time."

"Okay, let's consider it a done deal." Christian said. "When we get through with him, Enrique will wish he'd never heard of Port Serenity."

Chapter Twenty-Seven

The clatter of dishes was drowned out by the drone of conversation at Daisy's Diner, the best place on the Gulf Coast for biscuits and gravy. Lolly had chosen the place to break the news of her engagement, and now Olivia intended to reciprocate.

The news of Selena's kidnapping had put a temporary damper on her good mood. But there were a few people she couldn't wait to tell—namely her parents and Lolly. If they heard the good news through the grapevine she'd definitely be in the doghouse.

Olivia couldn't stop staring at her engagement ring. It was perfect—a brilliant ruby surrounded by diamonds. C.J. said it suited her better than a traditional ring.

Lolly and the twins arrived amid a flurry of "howdys" from the rest of the diners. She finally maneuvered the tandem stroller into place and fell into the booth.

"If we have any luck at all, they'll go to sleep. I

just fed them." As she pushed the stroller back and forth both children began to look droopy.

Lolly tucked a blanket under Renee's chin. "The little piglets will be milkshake junkies by the time they get to the first grade."

The milkshake thing had been their private joke for years. Lolly couldn't pass a Dairy Queen without whipping by the take-out window. Lord—the woman should weigh three hundred pounds but—but no, she looked like a movie star.

Olivia's left hand was on the table, covered with her right.

A tiny burp was the signal that both girls were off in Sandman Land, so Lolly grabbed a menu. "No telling how long they'll be asleep. I'd better order now."

Olivia waited patiently while her friend decided on lunch, then broached the subject. "I had an exciting experience over the weekend."

That got Lolly's attention. "What?"

"This." Olivia held her hand out.

"Ohmigod!" Lolly squealed. The twins both jerked awake and joined in the racket. "Ohmigod." Lolly repeated, but lowered the decibel level as she rocked the stroller. "Please tell me that's from C.J."

"Yep."

"Oh, sweetie, if I could get over there to hug you without disturbing these two—" she nodded at the twins "—I'd squeeze you to death. I can't believe it. I was beginning to think you weren't ever going to get together. Wait till I tell Christian. And *you* owe me a trip to Mexico." She smirked.

Olivia was smiling so much her cheeks hurt. "I'm going to run by the house this afternoon to tell Mom and Dad. I think they'll be pleased."

"Pleased! Are you nuts? They'll be tickled pink," Lolly announced, and Olivia suspected she was right.

"You back there, Mama?" Olivia called from the front hall, then made her way to the kitchen. "Smells wonderful in here." She lifted the lid on a huge pot.

"We're having gumbo," Rose said as she took a skillet of cornbread from the oven. "Are you staying for supper?"

"Sure." Olivia grabbed a carrot from the chopping block and took a big bite.

""What do you think?" When she presented her hand for inspection, Rose squealed at the top of her lungs.

Raul came skidding into the kitchen. "What's wrong?"

Rose had enveloped her daughter in a gigantic hug and was crying. "Look." She held up Olivia's hand. "She's engaged! About time. I'm going to have the chance to be a grandmother."

Babies were the last thing on Olivia's mind; she was still trying to decide how it had all happened. The next step after an engagement was a wedding, and that meant china patterns and bridesmaids.

Mother Mary! Was she ready for this?

Chapter Twenty-Eight

C.J. had waged a long debate with himself over what to tell Olivia about the Enrique plan, but honesty finally won. He just hoped the truth didn't bite him on the butt.

He had called Olivia's office hoping to catch her before she went home. "Livy darlin', I need to talk to you. Let's go to dinner."

Olivia quickly agreed to the date. "You're on. I've had a really rough day. But we have to go someplace that serves green stuff. Your eating habits are deplorable."

"That's because I've been a bachelor for years." He couldn't wait until he had someone to share dinner with on a permanent basis. Even grilled cheese sandwiches would be a delight if he shared them with Olivia.

Green and healthy were the criteria. His mom served vegetables with every meal, but her place wasn't an option for this conversation. The next best solution was Lindy's Cafeteria—they had the best fried okra and butterbeans in the county.

They gorged themselves on fried chicken, corn bread, mashed potatoes and collard greens before C.J. worked up the courage to initiate the topic he really wanted to discuss.

"Livy," he said as he dug into a bowl of banana pudding. Maybe some refined sugar would give him a boost of courage. "We've decided to take care of Enrique Bolivar. If we don't, Selena will never be safe. I've put as many men as I can on both you and Selena, but I can't provide twenty-four-hour-a-day bodyguards. Chandler's at home to watch Selena, so that's a stopgap. But we have to come up with a permanent solution."

"And how about me?" Olivia asked.

C.J. gave her one of his broadest grins. "You could move into my house or I could move into yours. Or I could spend every night at your house." He waggled his eyebrows suggestively.

Although they were engaged and she was sorely tempted, she couldn't quite make that leap. "I don't think so. Not right now." She knew her answer irritated him, but he managed to maintain his calm cop voice.

"And when will you be ready? Or were you planning to maintain separate houses after we get married."

That was a bit snide, but could she really blame him?

Olivia put her hand over his. "I love you, honestly I do. Just give me some time, okay?" When she stopped breaking out in hives whenever she thought about wedding invitations, everything would be A-okay—really it would.

His eyes crinkled in the beginnings of a grin. "Sure. But you can't blame a guy for trying."

Olivia wiped her mouth and set down her fork. "We'll work this out, I know we will. But for right this minute, let's return to the original subject. What do you mean you're going to do something about Bolivar?"

"Christian, Chandler and I have a plan. And I'll need you to babysit Fang."

"Certainly I'll keep him, I love him. And what do you mean, a plan?"

C.J. explained the proposed scenario, and when he finished Olivia was dumbfounded. What a harebrained, ingenious idea.

"And what happens if you idiots get caught?"

C.J. managed to look sheepish. "They'll throw us in jail and you'll have to come down and break us out."

"That's what I was afraid you were going to say." Lord in heaven, she loved that man, but the things he was willing to do were outlandish. She prayed he didn't get killed in Mexico.

Chapter Twenty-Nine

The interior of the cantina was dark and smelled of sweat, urine and years of spilled tequila. A haggard prostitute stopped C.J. and rubbed her breasts against his arm. The woman must be desperate—he was looking pretty skanky. He shook his head in response to her final shimmy and headed to the table where Christian was nursing a drink.

Christian nodded toward the whore, who had approached another potential customer. "Must be the biker look. Gets the girls every time." And he should know; he'd used it frequently during his undercover days.

C.J. ignored his comment. "Is everything ready?" he asked, even though Christian had been in Mexico for almost two weeks setting up the sting and C.J. knew he wouldn't leave anything to chance.

"Yep."

"What did you tell the captain?" C.J. asked, even though the answer was irrelevant.

"When I told him we had a plan to lure Enrique

Bolivar to Matamoros and then spirit him across the border, he didn't bat an eyelash. He simply asked if we'd informed our Mexican friends about this little party. When I told him no, he said, and I quote 'The less I know, the less I'll have to tell anyone who asks.' Then he kicked me out of his office."

Everything was falling into place. All they needed was the final puzzle piece—Enrique Bolivar.

C.J. leaned his chair back on two legs. Enrique had a child with a potentially fatal heart problem. Unfortunately, Enrique's empathy didn't extend to getting his son proper medical attention. Fortunately, that made the child's mother extremely receptive to the idea of helping C.J.

"The kid and his grandmother are already on their way to the specialty clinic in Alabama for his operation." Arranging that kind of medical attention had been no small feat.

"Can his mother really lure Bolivar up here?" Christian asked.

C.J. threw back a shot of tequila before he answered. "I'd bet my pension on it. Luna is Bolivar's cousin and his latest lover. And as we both know, he doesn't like to give away his possessions. That's why he has his boxers in such a twist over Selena, and it's why he'll follow Luna here."

"You don't think she'll double-cross us, do you?" Christian was pretty sure he knew the answer, but he wanted confirmation.

"No way. First of all, she's not that fond of Enrique, and more than anything she'd protect that kid of hers with her life. The whole family is planning to stay in Alabama after the operation."

Christian wondered whether the rickety chair would hold him if he tipped it back. "Brief me again on the story we're using for her trip to the border."

"She's supposed to be visiting her dying mother, but *mamacita* has mysteriously vanished. Strange how those women vanish into thin air," C.J. said and then contemplated the danger involved in this plan—both personally and professionally. Since it was a rogue mission, they'd be in a huge mess if they failed.

Chandler strolled in and took a seat. He was their logistics guy.

"Everything ready?" C.J. asked his brother.

Chandler made an okay sign with his fingers. "Let's get this show on the road."

The dingy alley smelled like rotting food. A barefoot child followed them, begging for money, gum and cigarettes. It was stupid, but C.J. couldn't resist. He handed the kid a few bucks and before long, they were surrounded by a horde of children ranging in age from two to fifteen.

"There's our ride." Chandler indicated a recent-model Volvo station wagon with a Matamoros policeman leaning against the front bumper. He gave the man a bill—a large bill—and the cop strolled off.

Chandler hit the automatic locks and the men climbed in to go to the rundown '50s-era motel that was their base of operation. It was situated on the southern edge of town and their rooms were at the far end of the complex, hidden by a screen of lush vegetation. The remote location and thick tropical foliage made it perfect for a kidnapping.

"Luna's already here and ready to go. She's a bit nervous, but as long as she can hold it together, I think we're okay," Chandler informed them as he killed the engine. C.J. hadn't spotted the highly effective group of Drug Enforcement agents Christian had recruited to take care of Bolivar's bodyguards. However, he was sure they were present. With those guys on the job, Enrique's goons would be expeditiously removed from the scene. One minute they'd be there, the next they'd be gone.

As soon as Bolivar entered the motel room he'd be completely on his own and that didn't bode well for his future freedom. C.J. hated involving Luna in this operation but if it was the only way he could free Selena from the hell her life had become, he'd do it.

C.J. stepped into the room and was assailed by a blast of frigid air and the overpowering odor of moldy carpet. The air-conditioning was a welcome relief from the oppressive heat; as for the stale smell—they wouldn't stick around long enough to die from toxic mold.

"You might want to get dressed while we wait." Chandler tossed him a pile of clothing.

With a mere change of clothes, C.J. suddenly became a yuppie—Docksiders (no socks), Polo (with an embroidered horse on the pocket) and khaki shorts. Who said clothes didn't make the man?

Waiting was the hard part—keeping the adrena-

line under control, anticipating each move, and waiting. It was almost an hour before they heard anything
other than background noise on the listening devices
they'd planted in the room next door. Then they
heard Enrique Bolivar's voice. The curtain on this
drama was about to go up and C.J.'s crew was ready.
He touched the 9mm Beretta tucked in the back
waistband of his shorts.

The woman greeted her visitor and there was a
period of silence.

"The goodbye kiss," Christian commented. "Too
bad the sucker doesn't know it will be the last one
he gets for a long, long time."

When they heard Bolivar excuse himself to go to
the bathroom, C.J. silently opened the adjoining door
and felt a surge of sympathy for the woman standing
by the bed. Luna looked like a deer caught in the head-
lights, but regardless of her terror, or maybe because
of it, she managed to scamper into their room. From
there one of the DEA guys would take her across the
border and send her on to her son in Alabama.

Bolivar was focused on taking care of business
and missed the fact that he had company—until
Christian pumped a load of anesthetic into his arm.
He made a choking sound and attempted a futile
grab for his gun before dropping like a rock.

"Watch him, and I'll get his new wardrobe," C.J.
instructed as he returned to the adjoining room to
retrieve the bag he had stashed.

By the time C.J. came back with the items they
needed to transform Enrique into a drunken com-

puter salesman, Christian had him stripped. On went the shorts, off went the scraggly beard—and on went the University of Texas ball cap.

"What do you think?" C.J. asked as he stepped back to admire the transformation.

"I think the border guards would have to be blind to buy this one," Christian admitted rather reluctantly. "But we'll make it work. We have to."

Chandler had the audacity to smile. "Or maybe they'll need the right incentive." He rubbed his thumb and forefinger together in the universal symbol for money. "And I've taken care of that bribe."

C.J. nodded, knowing his brother had done what was necessary to smooth the way. "Do you have the extra syringe?" he asked.

"Right here." Christian produced a capped needle from his pocket. "And here's the booze." He poured a liberal portion into Bolivar's mouth and then tilted him to let it run on to the floor. "Don't want him to drown on this stuff, do we?" If things worked out as planned, this would be the last time Señor Bolivar breathed the fresh air of freedom.

Two DEA men were waiting outside with the Volvo. They threw Bolivar in the back seat, while C.J. and Christian jumped in to bracket him.

"Whew! Could someone crank up the air conditioner? The smell on this guy could knock over an elephant," Christian complained as he shifted Bolivar's face toward C.J. "How long do you think he'll be out?" he asked Chandler, who had provided the sedative.

"Long enough," Chandler answered and then

handed Christian the liquor bottle before he got into the driver's seat. "Rinse your mouth out," he instructed. "We have to all smell like booze. That is, everyone but me. I'm your designated driver."

C.J. was astonished his brother was risking a stay in a Mexican jail for someone he supposedly didn't like. Uh-huh—sure!

Their plan was to go through the border crossing posing as a group of high-flying Texans on a bachelor party to end all parties. Two days of drinking, strippers—the full-meal deal.

Traffic slowed and came to a stop as the lights of the Mexican/U.S. border lit up the night sky. The U.S. immigration folks would be harder to fool than the Mexican *Federales,* especially since some money had strategically changed hands on the southern side of the border. But it still wouldn't be a walk in the park.

As the traffic queue inched closer to the Mexican checkpoint C.J. could see that on the American side some cars were pulled over for a detailed inspection. The officials were looking for drugs, untaxed booze and terrorists. And although this was a highly illegal operation, they didn't fit the profile. If luck was with them, and if the stars were all properly aligned, they'd be able to slide through with minimal interrogation.

And then it happened.

Out of the corner of his eye, C.J. spotted something so out of place it made the hair stand up on the back of his neck. "Crap!" C.J. muttered and nudged Christian. "Do you see what I see?"

Christian glanced toward the Mexican guard shack and immediately spied a SWAT team—all decked out in Kevlar; obviously they were waiting for something or someone. He just hoped it wasn't them!

"I'd say we'd better start saying a few Hail Marys," Christian mumbled. They were sitting ducks if the dudes in black were after them. Even though they all had hidden weapons, they weren't about to get involved in a firefight.

"Stay calm," C.J. said, although he knew the warning wasn't necessary. These guys were as professional as they came.

They inched forward, expecting the worst, hoping for the best. It was finally their turn to approach the Mexican policeman, but he stepped in front of the car and stopped their forward motion.

Then all hell broke loose. Thank goodness it was aimed at the car on their left. When the chaos died down, four men were kissing the asphalt. And it wasn't them!

"That's enough to make you need a clean pair of drawers," the DEA agent in the front seat whispered. And wasn't that the truth.

It took almost an hour for the traffic to resume its crawl north. Inch by agonizing inch they moved forward.

When they reached the Mexican policeman, he leaned in the driver's side window and briefly looked over the five men. After a perfunctory glance at their IDs, he waved them through. Another obstacle down, but the hardest was yet to come. Talk about anticlimactic.

The Volvo rolled up to the U.S. checkpoint. Inside the guard post, one INS officer ran their license plate while the men outside conducted hands-on inspections of cars as they streamed across the border. Thousands of people used this bridge every day for work, play and smuggling operations.

A man in a khaki uniform leaned into the window. "May I see some ID from all you gentlemen?" Talk about a question for which there was only one acceptable answer.

Chandler whipped out his passport almost as fast as he kicked into his thick Texas drawl. "Sure 'nuf. Here you go. Now the fella in the back's kinda three sheets to the wind—you know what I mean," he whispered as if they were best friends. "He's gettin' married and we took him out to have one last fling. I'm driving 'cause I don't drink, but the rest of these fellas are in bad shape."

At the declaration, Christian let out an earthshaking belch. Everyone in the car, with the exception of Bolivar, was praying their fake IDs would stand the test of two separate border inspections.

The border guard appeared doubtful as he checked the pile of IDs they had handed him. He motioned over another man who glanced into the car and then checked the paperwork before he waved them through.

C.J. didn't realize he'd been holding his breath. If the guards on either side of the border had called their bluff, they'd have been in a pile of trouble. But they'd actually made it through.

After they were safely in the U.S., Chandler pulled the car over and high-fived Christian and C.J.

"As soon as we get to Harlingen, we'll anonymously dump our friend with the authorities and make ourselves scarce," C.J. said, repeating their plan. If they'd been caught, the entire law enforcement world would have disavowed them. But they'd been successful, and not only would this scum cease to be a problem for Selena, he would face justice. With his outstanding warrants, Enrique would be lucky to make it out of jail before the age of ninety.

Now C.J. had to turn a laser focus on the situation with Olivia and her unknown assailant.

Chapter Thirty

C.J. had been in Mexico almost a week and Olivia was antsy about getting him home. The deputy sitting outside her house and the vet clinic was reassuring, but just the idea of having a babysitter irritated her. She'd much rather have C.J. guard her body.

Her vet tech had called in sick, so she was staying late to check the post-op patients. Dr. Bob had volunteered, but it was his bowling night and Olivia sent him off. Not only was it a good way to make points with her boss, it was a great excuse to skip Rose's latest Sara Belle party. Heaven help the female population of Port Serenity—her mother had been snookered into becoming a Sara Belle distributor. Please God, that phase of Mama's life would end soon—Olivia had about had it with stuffed mushrooms and sherbet punch.

A trio of barking dogs greeted her as she opened the kennel door. It was as dark as the inside of a well; the only illumination was the exit sign. So it came as a huge surprise when she bounced off an obviously male body. Big uh-oh. Then she felt the gun in her ribs. Pulleeze—not again.

"Eeeyyaaa!" Olivia screamed at the top of her lungs. The unexpected screech startled her assailant into dropping his arm for a brief but valuable moment. Time to beat feet. Olivia sprinted to her office intending to barricade herself in and call for help— if the phone lines weren't cut. But she had a cell phone in her purse. She could only hope she'd recharged the stupid thing.

Olivia slammed through the swinging door and heard a grunt of pain when it flew back and into the man's face. Deep down she hoped the jerk had a broken nose, not that she was a violent person or anything like that.

Fifteen more feet to her office, fifteen more feet to a cell phone that might or might not be charged, fifteen more feet to safety—but she didn't make it even two feet before he grabbed her ponytail and pulled her to a screeching halt. Damn, damn, double damn, that hurt.

On to Plan B—but what *was* Plan B? Kick him in the nuts, gouge his eyes out or give him an elbow in the gut. Then she saw the cage where Myrtie the giant python was napping and she had a white-hot, mind-searing stroke of genius. Myrtie was huge, scary and best of all—Myrtie was a *snake*. Olivia happened to know she was a sweetie, but she scared the piddle out of just about everyone.

Olivia reached into the glass cage and grabbed the reptile's head. She prayed this idiot wasn't the one person in a thousand who actually liked long, scaly, cold-blooded creatures. Myrtie was too heavy to get her totally out of her aquarium, but Olivia had her hands around enough of Myrtie's body to poke the head of the sleeping reptile in her pursuer's face. When Myrtie flicked her forked tongue, the idiot let out a primal scream and scrambled for the exit. Thank God! He wasn't a snake lover.

Olivia stuffed Myrtie back into her glass home. Her rubbery knees barely carried her to the office where she immediately pushed the filing cabinet in front of the door. Fang writhed around her ankles, barking and panting. Great—she wasn't the only one about to hyperventilate. C.J. wasn't answering his cell, so she did the next best thing and called 911.

CHANDLER AND C.J. were still basking in the euphoria of a job well done when they pulled into Corrine's driveway. Barring any complications, Enrique Bolivar wouldn't bother anyone for at least a decade. It might not have been the most legal action the brothers had ever taken, but they'd accomplished something every drug agency in the country had tried and failed to do. Another bad guy was off the street and Selena could breathe a sigh of relief.

C.J. cut the engine and turned to Chandler. "Thanks. We couldn't have done it without you." This was about as close as the brothers would get to a hug.

Chandler smiled. "My pleasure. Now maybe Selena can get on with her life."

"I've been meaning to ask you, but I wasn't completely sure you wouldn't punch me in the nose. What's up with you two?"

Chandler was deep in thought. "I'm not sure. Physically—nothing. Mentally—we have this killer love/hate relationship." He laughed ruefully. "You ought to know how it is. I'm desperately trying to squelch my lascivious ideas. You might not have noticed, but she hates me."

C.J. was about to refute that statement when he was interrupted by his cell phone. "Baker here," he answered.

"C.J." Olivia tried not to sound hysterical, but she wasn't very successful.

"What's wrong, sweetheart?"

"He…he…he," she sniffed and then broke into sobs.

"Slow down. Take a deep breath," C.J. said gently. "And tell me what happened."

"Someone broke into the clinic."

"Just wait there. Are you all right?" A surge of panic almost overwhelmed him. "Lock your office door. I'll be there in two minutes."

In the background he could hear a man's voice. "Is that one of my deputies?"

"Yeah. I'm okay, just scared. I think the knocking is my bodyguard."

"Don't answer. Let me contact the dispatcher and make sure it's legit." He sprinted to the Explorer to use the radio. When he confirmed that it was his deputy trying to get into the vet clinic, he hit the siren and sped to Olivia.

A veteran NASCAR driver couldn't have done

better. C.J. skidded into the parking lot and was out of the Explorer almost before he'd slammed the transmission into Park. The flashing red-and-blue lights of Deputy Cunningham's cruiser bounced off the white walls.

C.J. followed the sound of voices to Olivia's office and took her into his arms. "Livy, I about freaked out." His first inclination was to pat down every square inch of her body, but since there were two deputies watching, he ruled out that idea.

He kept his arm around her shoulders, but addressed his men. "Find anything?"

"Nope, boss. Not a thing other than the fact that he picked the lock on the back door. There are also some tire prints in the next field over. We're figuring he had an accomplice."

Deputy Cunningham recited the details of his initial investigation. He was obviously curious about the relationship between C.J. and Olivia.

"Get some techs out and dust everything." C.J. instructed them and then turned to address Olivia. "Was he wearing gloves?"

She was holding Fang, who was squirming madly. "Heavens, he could've been wearing Mickey Mouse ears and I wouldn't have noticed." She told him about the part Myrtie had played in her near miss.

"You threatened him with a snake!" He tapped lightly on the glass wall of the aquarium. "Good Myrtie." He took the dog from her arms and was immediately bathed in kisses.

Chapter Thirty-One

C.J. didn't know whether it was the full moon or the unseasonably hot weather—you could almost wring the water out of the air—but whatever it was, the crazies were out in force. The Hardaways had mysteriously disappeared from the face of the earth and the guys on motorcycles were as elusive as ever. Plus now he had a break-in at Rose Alvarado's gallery. What next?

Should he tell Olivia? Yep—it wasn't smart to keep secrets from that young lady.

"Livy, do you know where your parents are?" he asked. Rose's gallery had an alarm and that was probably the only thing that had stopped the intruders. The deputies had turned off the noisy system, but so far they hadn't located Rose or Raul.

"Why?" she asked.

Bless her heart, she had a suspicious streak a mile wide.

He tipped back his Stetson, one of his favorite stalling tactics. "Because someone tried to break into the Toad and Turtle and we can't get in touch with Rose. I'd like her to take an inventory and secure the place."

"Mother Mary! This used to be a nice place to live. What has *happened* to this town?"

That was exactly what C.J. intended to find out.

Olivia tried both her mother's cell and her home phone, to no avail. "I'm pretty sure she has a Sara Belle party at Sissy's house. And I think Daddy's bowling."

"Do you know Sissy's number?"

"No."

"That's okay, I can find it." C.J. got the number for Lolly's aunt from the dispatcher—but he didn't get an answer when he called.

"Let's go see if we can get hold of her."

"WHAT DO YOU THINK is really going on?" Olivia asked. The blue lights of the dash emphasized C.J.'s clenched jaw.

She reached across the mounted computer and touched his forearm. "I'm scared." It was the first time she'd admitted that the situation was beyond her control. "It can't be money. I'm still knee-deep in paying off my loans. And they couldn't have heard about the jar of pennies I've saved since the eighth grade." She put her head in her hands. "This is making me crazy!"

"I know, sweetheart." C.J. stroked her cheek. "I'll be honest, I don't have a clue. But I certainly intend to find out. I think it has something to do with the Hardaways, but I don't know what. I did a background check on them and didn't learn anything other than the fact that he's an itinerant preacher from Arizona. They don't have rap sheets or finger-prints or anything."

He wouldn't leave a stone unturned while some-one was trying to harm the woman he loved. "After we talk to your mom and get that settled, I'll take the rest of the night off. Come stay with me. I'm feelin' the need to hold you." He ran his finger gently across her bottom lip.

The coup de grâce to the miniseduction was a wink—an irresistible enticement.

"Uh-huh." A night with C.J. would certainly get her mind off assailants and felons. What was it about the man that made her turn to mush every time he touched her?

He had the temerity to grin. "I presume that's a yes." Before she could respond, they'd arrived in Sissy's neighborhood.

"Guess we were right. Look at all the cars."

The street was lined with familiar autos. It seemed that every woman in town over the age of forty-five was at the Sara Belle party. "These parties are simply an excuse to gossip and drink," Olivia pronounced. Not that there was anything wrong with sharing a glass of good wine and a few rumors with friends.

C.J. found a parking spot at the end of the block. With his police vehicle he could have double-parked, but he didn't think this situation warranted it.

Sissy was decked out in a pink satin robe and fluffy matching mules when she answered the door.

"Mrs. Aguirre, ma'am." C.J. tipped his hat. "Is

Rose available? I need to speak to her." Sissy's frightened glance bounced from C.J. to Olivia. She didn't utter a word before she scurried to the living room, leaving them standing on the porch.

"Guess we scared her," C.J. commented as he ushered Olivia into the foyer and closed the front door. "Finding a cop on your doorstep at night tends to prompt that reaction."

Rose Alvarado ran up to Olivia and almost knocked her over with her hug. "What's wrong? Is it your daddy?"

"No, Mama. Daddy's fine, I'm sure. Someone tried to break into the gallery and you need to come with us to check it out. It was probably kids." And if her mother bought that load of garbage, pigs would soon be doing barrel rolls over Port Serenity.

The gallery office was ransacked, but as far as they could tell nothing else was taken or disturbed. "Do you have anything valuable that someone might want?" C.J. asked.

Rose was at the desk trying to restore order to the chaos.

"No. I don't keep money overnight and the jewelry is in the safe. The only other valuable thing in here is the computer system. And as you can see—" she waved a hand at the equipment "—it's all here. I don't get it."

Neither did C.J. First someone tried to assault Olivia, and then Rose's gallery was ransacked. Either the two women had something in their possession, or someone had a vendetta against the family. And the

Alvarado family was about as wholesome as you could get.

"Has anyone given you anything in the past couple of months? Asked you to keep a diary, a book, a piece of jewelry for them? Think outside the box. It could be anything."

Olivia nibbled on her bottom lip as she contemplated the question. "I can't come up with anything." She turned to her mother. "How about you?"

Rose had an identical response. "Do you *really* think they're looking for something?" she asked C.J.

"Yes, ma'am. I sure do." And C.J. knew he'd better discover it sooner rather than later.

Chapter Thirty-Two

"I still can't figure out why someone would do all this…." Olivia said as she gestured helplessly trying to come up with the appropriate word. After C.J. and Olivia left the gallery, they picked up takeout from the deli and had supper on C.J.'s deck. Fang was chewing on a dried pig's ear.

Olivia was spooned up against C.J.'s chest as they sat on the chaise. "Mmm. This feels so good. I love listening to the ocean."

"Me, too." He emphasized his agreement with a kiss on her neck. "For tonight, let's forget about bad guys and concentrate on us."

"Oh, yes." It was hard to concentrate when he was nibbling on her neck. Not to mention the things he was doing with his hands—those talented, talented hands.

He worked his kisses down from her neck to her collarbone and back across the nape of her neck.

"You can keep that up for a century, if you like."

"Yeah, I like," he muttered as he skimmed kisses

on every square inch of uncovered skin. His hands had moved under her T-shirt to caress her breasts.

Olivia snuggled in closer and raised her arms around his neck. "Hmm," she purred, contentment coming from every pore.

"I know something that'll make you feel even better."

"Better than this? No way."

"Yeah, way." He scooted Olivia forward enough on the chaise for him to get up. "Come with me." He gave her a hand up and led her back to the master bedroom.

"Your bed, huh?"

"Nope." He pulled her into the bathroom and turned on the water in the Jacuzzi. "I've been waiting to christen this tub with you." C.J. rummaged through the linen closet and brought out a bottle of lavender-scented bubble bath. "And for you, I don't even mind smelling like a bawdy house."

His waggling eyebrow pushed Olivia into a bout of the giggles. She had never mastered the art of waggling an eyebrow.

"So you don't mind smelling like a girl, huh?" She wrapped her arms around his neck and rubbed up and down—a contented kitten couldn't have done it better.

"Too many clothes," he mumbled between hot, wet kisses. Her T-shirt went sailing to the floor. His ended up on the same pile.

The sudsy water filled the tub and bubbled like the witches' cauldron in *Macbeth*. She rubbed her hands against the plane of his chest and ran a finger down to the button fly on his Levi's. Pop went the first. Pop went the second. When she reached the third, his hand covered hers.

"It's your turn." He slowly, slowly, slowly pulled down the zipper of her Wranglers, then slid off her jeans and sandals.

He pulled her closer to the bathtub as he dispensed with his jeans, then took her hand and they stepped in.

There was nothing more erotic than a tub of hot water and an even hotter man. And this man was about as hot as you could get.

Olivia sank into the warm water while drinking in the sight of those mesmerizing sea-foam-green eyes, the dimples that could charm the hardest of hearts—and had she mentioned the most awesome chest west of the Mississippi?

He held out his hand, which contained a bar of soap. "Do you want me to wash your back?"

"Uh-huh." Olivia drifted over and presented her back for his devious form of soaping. Up and down, round and round—the massaging was interspersed with small nibbles every place he rinsed off the soap. Then he drew her closer and did the same to the front—deliberately paying rapt attention to her sensitive nipples.

"You're killing me!" Not only was she red-hot with lust, her entire body had turned into a bowl of Jell-O. Her legs wouldn't hold her up even if the place caught fire. "Do something," she demanded.

The chuckle rumbled up from his belly. "Do what?" he said innocently, knowing full well what she wanted.

"This!" Olivia lunged for him, capturing his mouth in a kiss that went on and on.

"MY FINGERS ARE AS wrinkled as raisins." Olivia lifted a hand for his inspection. "Why don't we adjourn to the bed?"

"Sounds like a plan to me." C.J. stood and took Olivia with him. "Wait here." He stepped out of the tub, returned with a fluffy white bathrobe and made a ceremony of wrapping it around her.

"Do you keep this for all your women?" It was an unfair question, but one her evil angel forced her to ask.

He kissed her once and then repeated it before he retrieved a matching robe from the back of the door. "Nope. I'm an optimist. I knew you'd be here."

Chapter Thirty-Three

The truce between Chandler and Selena was short-lived. She had hoped their dinner in Corpus would be a turning point—but so much for unfounded optimism.

After the Mexican encounter with Enrique, Chandler had reverted to monosyllabic communication. Yes, no, maybe—and sometimes if she was lucky he'd throw in a "pass the salt."

The silent treatment was apparently irritating Corrine, too, because at dinner she asked him when he was planning to return to New York. That was about as subtle as a Mack truck.

Selena wasn't quite sure what she thought about Chandler going back to work. But she did know that since Enrique was out of the picture, she had to decide what to do with the rest of her life. Did she want to live in Dallas again? That wasn't very appealing. What *did* she want to do?

Corrine was at a biker picnic and Chandler was God only knew where—so the hell with him. Selena was fixing a tuna salad sandwich when she heard the front door open. Since Enrique was indisposed, so to speak, it was either Chandler or the local burglar, and at this point Selena didn't know which was preferable.

Chandler strolled in and took a big bite of her sandwich.

"Stop that!" Selena swatted his hand and indicated the bowl of tuna. "Make your own."

Even his smirk was sexy. "It's easier to snack on yours," he replied, but he gave her the remainder of the sandwich.

"Keep it. I'll make another one."

"Suit yourself." He put the sandwich on a plate and loaded it up with potato chips. Chandler truly didn't know why he turned into a Neanderthal every time he encountered Selena, but when he got a whiff of her shampoo something hit him like a ton of bricks. It was lust—pure and simple and if it *wasn't* lust he was in a boatload of trouble.

"What are you planning to do now that Enrique isn't on your tail?" He might as well ask the question that had been niggling at him.

She plopped a spoonful of tuna onto a bed of lettuce and sat down to eat. "I have to get a job. Money's getting a bit scarce and I can't sponge off your family forever." She wasn't about to confide in him. "How about you?"

Chandler chuckled, thinking about his mother's questioning. "Mom says it's time for me to go back to work. I'm pretty sure all the old *Star Trek* reruns are driving her nuts."

Selena could relate to that—if she never heard Captain Kirk's voice again, she'd be a happy woman.

"Perhaps."

"Perhaps?" Suddenly he moved his chair so close that if she leaned over just a bit she could kiss him—not that she would ever consider kissing him. Uh-huh—sure!

Chandler had been the starring attraction in a number of serious fantasies, but they didn't even compare to the real thing. She was in his arms before she had a chance to offer even token resistance. The kiss was long and thorough, and the stray thought skittered through her brain that he wasn't as immune as he'd always pretended. In fact, he didn't seem impervious at all.

"Chandler," Selena murmured when he finished a scrumptious foray of her mouth.

"Hmm."

"Do you think this is wise?" She wasn't sure why she was broaching this particular subject.

"Hmm."

Okay, so he was engrossed in what he was doing—which wasn't such a bad idea.

"Oh, Selena." Chandler buried his face in the hollow of her neck and sifted her hair through his fingers. "I've wanted to do this for weeks."

That was an interesting admission. Selena placed a hand on his chest and gently pushed. "So why have you been at my throat since you've been here?" What *was* wrong with her? Kissing Chandler had been an obsession for practically her entire adult life—so why was she sabotaging her one, and probably only, chance?

"What?"

Yep—he'd skipped from lust to mad in a record one point two seconds, and it was her own fault.

"I simply wondered why you were interested in kissing me now." And when had she mastered the snooty debutante attitude?

Chandler shoved back his chair and stood. "I don't think I'm interested anymore." He ran a hand through his hair. "No, make that I'm sure I'm not interested, now or ever. Why would I get involved with someone who could jump in and out of marriage as casually as you did?"

"What did you say?" Selena came to her feet, ready to take on the man of her fantasies who had somehow changed into her worst nightmare.

"I'm talking about you getting married in order to have a better lifestyle. That's about as cheap as you can get." Good God! Where had that come from? He was known for thinking on his feet, but this time his brain had taken a vacation.

"Cheap? I'll give you cheap! *Madre de Dios!*" she screeched, very tempted to whack him in the face with a handful of tuna salad. Instead, she ran out of the kitchen.

"I must be the biggest idiot in the universe," Chandler muttered to himself. How could he have made such a mess of things? Selena probably wouldn't forgive him, and he couldn't blame her. He'd have a hard time forgiving himself.

Chapter Thirty-Four

Olivia's thoughts were such a jumble that keeping her mind on her job was almost impossible. Toward the end of the afternoon, C.J. called and said he had a meeting with the county exec and that he'd be over later that night. That was okay, because it gave her a chance to discuss the ongoing puzzle with Rose.

"MAMA, ARE YOU HOME?" Olivia called out. Rose's car was in the driveway, but the house was dark. Although it was suppertime, the stove was cold. The fragrant aromas that usually greeted her were merely a memory. Darn it! She'd been looking forward to fried chicken or lasagna.

Olivia grabbed a Coke and wandered into the family room assuming her mother would be home soon. A family conference was long overdue. If, as C.J. suspected, the attacks had happened because of something they had in their possession, they'd better figure out what it was—PDQ.

Olivia was halfway through a *Buffy* rerun when

she heard the telltale sounds of a key in the door. Betting it was her mother, she called out, "Mama, I'm in the family room."

"Be there in a minute, baby," Rose answered. Muffled noises came from the front foyer. Uh-oh. Someone had been shopping and wanted to hide the evidence. Olivia slipped into the hall to check her theory. Yep, Rose was surrounded by a pile of colorful department store bags and she was rummaging in the bottom of the closet to make room for the booty.

"Buy anything interesting?" Olivia loved to shop, but with all the recent craziness she hadn't taken time to indulge in that favorite hobby. A pair of new shoes might improve her mood—but then again, this was more momentous than a new pair of shoes.

Rose hugged her daughter. "You can look at everything but the stuff in the Foley's sack. Someone I know needs a special treat."

Olivia had always loved the "no particular reason" gifts Rose gave her.

"What did you get me?" Olivia squealed.

"You'll find out after I have some tea." Rose picked up the bag and marched toward her bedroom. "Rummage around in the kitchen and find some sweets. I'll be right back."

Olivia wandered back to the kitchen to pour her mom a glass of tea. If she was really lucky there'd be some homemade chocolate chip cookies. Everyone knew chocolate was brain food, and if they had a chance in h-e-double-toothpicks of figuring out this puzzle, they'd need a trainload of Snickers.

Olivia's search of the kitchen was interrupted by the doorbell. If luck was on her side, it was some kid selling candy. In that case she'd whip out a twenty and solve two problems with one purchase.

The doorbell pealed again. "Hold your horses," she called as she put down the glass of tea. "I'm coming." Olivia opened the door without peeking through the side window.

Good heavens, it was Florene Hardaway. "I heard you'd moved," she blurted. The rumor Olivia had heard was that as soon as the good preacher got out of the hospital they'd taken off. And good riddance— something about that woman raised the hair on the back of her neck.

"Can I come in?" Florene asked, by which time she was already halfway through the door. Pushy broad!

"Sure." Olivia stepped aside and took notice of her guest's appearance. Florene had always been flamboyant, but wow, she was sluttier than normal! Her massive cleavage was barely covered by a stretchy tube top that left her stomach bare. Yech! And her hair! What could be said about her hair other than it was the size of Mt. Vesuvius.

"Mama, Miz Hardaway is here," she yelled. The bimbo was Mama's guest. *She* could get rid of her!

"Please have a seat." Olivia followed Florene into the family room. The woman was as skittery as a virgin on her wedding night.

Olivia was fresh out of conversation topics. "How's your husband?"

"Thanks for asking. He's fine."

So much for small talk. "Would you like a glass of tea?" Darn those good manners—they popped up at the most inconvenient times.

"No, no. But do you have anything stronger?"

Stronger! This was totally weird.

"I don't know. Let me see what Daddy has."

Raul Alvarado's liquor supply consisted of half a bottle of tequila (no worm) and a dusty bottle of Grand Marnier.

"Tequila or Grand Marnier?" Olivia held up the two containers.

Florene didn't hesitate a second. "Tequila, straight up."

"Mama!" Olivia shouted. Rose could take care of this fruitcake. "Mama!"

"Olivia Alvarado, I'm not deaf. What's all the racket?" Rose spoke before she saw their visitor. "Florene, my word! What are you doing back in town?" When she saw the empty tequila bottle on the shelf and the glass of clear liquid in Florene's hand, she shot Olivia a puzzled look.

Olivia responded with a shrug.

"I see you have some refreshment. Should I open a bottle of wine?" Rose asked without waiting for an answer. Lickety split—she was in the kitchen snatching the cork out of a bottle of Chardonnay, apparently she was working on the assumption that it was five o'clock somewhere in the world.

That was just fine. Olivia suspected before the end of this encounter they'd both need more than a single glass of wine. And was her premonition spot on.

Rose gave Olivia a tumbler of wine. "Here, I think you'll need this."

"Okay, Florene. What's up?" Rose asked.

The woman wiped her hands down the front of her skintight Wranglers, played with the tassels on a throw pillow and twisted and twirled her hair in an obvious stalling tactic. If her florid complexion was any indication, her blood pressure was in the stratosphere.

"Well, it's like this." Florene bit her lip nervously. "Um, I really didn't intend to get you folks involved." She held out her hands in supplication. "But everything got screwed up."

Olivia wanted to scream in exasperation, but managed to maintain her calm. Mama didn't appear to be faring as well.

"Go on, go on." Rose gulped half her glass of Chardonnay.

"It's like this," she said again. "My name's not Florene Hardaway and my husband is not Brother Wilbur of the Bayou Church of the Saved Sinners. In fact," she sheepishly admitted, "before we got to Port Serenity, we hadn't darkened the door of a church in almost twenty years."

Okay, in a month of surprises that had to be the granddaddy.

"My name is Yvonne Madden and my hubby is Mad Dog Madden. He was one of the big dogs," she giggled at the pun, "of the Diablo biker gang from New Mexico. That is, until Pit Viper, he's the head guy you know, got all wrapped around the axle about some missing money. Swear to God—" she made the scouting salute of three fingers "—we didn't know nothin' about that money. But we decided it was time to make ourselves scarce."

Olivia and Rose listened intently, unsure why this revelation had anything to do with them.

"But as a bit of insurance we took a computer disk that has all the Diablo drug contacts, bank account numbers, stuff that could send a lot of people to the pen in Santa Fe."

O-kay! This had jumped from weird to downright bizarre. Olivia still couldn't figure out how this affected them. What did Florene want from them?

"I'll probably regret this, but I have to know. What happened to the real Reverend and Mrs. Hardaway?" Olivia asked.

"Oh, that's simple. We were on our way to Mexico when we stopped at the I-37 rest stop. You know the one way out in the boondocks? Anyway, Mad Dog's bike was making a funny noise, so we pulled in there. It was the middle of the night, but there was this old beat-up car sitting out there running." She finished off the glass of tequila.

"We could see there were two people in the car and they didn't look none too good. So Mad Dog jimmied the door, and sure enough, they were dead as mackerels. For about a second we considered calling the cops but then we remembered Mad Dog's rap sheet." Florene—no, make that Yvonne—leaned forward as if to let them in on a secret. "Cops don't look too favorable on a criminal record and dead bodies. Not that Mad Dog's ever done nothin' too violent.

"Anyway, those folks had everything but the kitchen sink in that car. That was because they were moving down here, you know. We found personal papers and letters from the church, plus their house keys. They made it easy for us to take over their lives. We started thinkin' that since we were close to the same age and size as the dead people, we'd take it as a sign from God. If we could hide out for a couple days, maybe a week, as Florene and Wilbur, it'd give us a head start on Pit Viper's boys." She paused for a breath. "So there you go. We were reborn as the Hardaways.

"Problem was we had to get rid of the real Hardaways. Then Mad Dog had this great idea. We'd dump them out at that wildlife place and let the critters eat the bodies. Too bad those gators didn't help us out. But that's neither here nor there." Yvonne waved a hand in the air. "Anyways, it worked pretty good until my dolt of a husband called an old buddy and Pit Viper got wind of where we were. He sent some guys down here to get the disk. So we had to leave." She apparently thought this was a satisfactory explanation, immediately flopped back and sighed.

They weren't murderers, but they were on a first-name basis with some biker dude named Pit Viper. Good Lord. And how did they manage the logistics of assuming someone's identity?

"How did you make sure you didn't meet someone from your past?"

"Well, we never took any phone calls and we had a message on the church machine that we'd get back to any callers. A few people phoned, but we never replied. We planned all along that this would be temporary."

"So what do you want from us?" Olivia asked.

"It's the pink piggy bank. You know the one I gave you the night of the first Sara Belle party? The computer disk I told you about is in that stupid pig. I had to hide it someplace, so I gave it to you as a hostess gift. We figured we'd rob your place and retrieve it before we left town But we had a few problems."

She had the grace to at least look guilty before she continued with her explanation. "When Pit Viper's boys beat up on Wilbur, he told them about you and the pig. And that's why they've been giving you guys such a hard time. I'm sorry about that. Really I am."

Rose looked as stricken as Olivia felt.

"Didn't you—" Before Rose could finish her question, Olivia grabbed her purse and fished out her cell phone.

"Yeah, I gave it to Amanda." She punched in Lolly's number, but Mee Maw answered.

"I'm babysitting. Lolly and Christian went to Corpus Christi for dinner." She was about to launch into a full-scale discussion of dining establishments on the Gulf Coast, but Olivia cut her off.

"Does Amanda still have that piggy bank I gave her?

"She does? Okay, listen…" Olivia could hear a discussion in the background. "I can't explain right now. But I want you to lock all the doors and not open them for anyone without a badge. I'll be there in ten minutes to get that bank." She didn't give Marcela a chance to respond before she punched the off button.

"I don't know whether you came here to retrieve the disk or not," Olivia said, "but I intend to take it to the sheriff." How dare these idiots endanger the lives of innocent people!

Florene didn't bat an eyelash at Olivia's pronouncement. "I figured you would. But I had to warn you before someone got hurt. Now my conscience is clear and we're gonna disappear for good." She picked up her purse and dashed for the front door.

"Oh, my heavens!" Rose clutched her chest. "Retrieve that thing immediately and take it to C.J. He'll know what to do with it."

OLIVIA BROKE EVERY SPEED LIMIT on her way to Lolly's. She'd probably scared Marcela out of a year's worth of life, but the sooner the pink beast and its contents were in the hands of a guy with a gun, the better she'd like it.

Marcela was standing at the back door when Olivia skidded in and stopped on a dime.

"Livy, child, you about scared me to death. I've got this place locked up like Fort Knox. Get in, get in." Mee Maw pulled Olivia in and slammed the dead bolt shut.

"What's this all about?" she demanded.

Olivia gave her a rundown on everything she knew. Even though she didn't think the thugs would target Lolly's house, she suggested Marcela call Christian and Lolly and tell them to come home.

"The bank is in Amanda's room on her dresser. I took her over to Leslie's house. It's lucky she's not here." Yes, that was a lucky break and they needed some luck.

She flew into her goddaughter's room and immediately saw the porker. Talk about butt-ugly. Marcela was on the phone explaining things to Lolly when Olivia whizzed out the door and jumped into her 'Vette.

It was a twenty-minute trip to C.J.'s beach house—but she intended to make it in ten. Petunia was feelin' the need to be in police custody.

Chapter Thirty-Five

C.J. was on the deck enjoying a cold beer and the sea breeze. He'd had a long, boring meeting with the board of county commissioners and needed some down time. The month had been a roller coaster of events and emotions. Enrique Bolivar was out of the picture, so Selena was safe. And his tenacity had paid off—Olivia had agreed to become a permanent part of his life, even though she was stalling on a wedding date. Now he had to keep *her* safe, and to do that he had to discover how Rose and Olivia were tied into the vandalism and break-ins.

His options were fairly limited. More than likely they had something in their possession. But what was it? Incessant banging on the front door brought his internal brainstorming to a halt.

"I'm coming," he yelled, but even though he was shouting he wasn't sure he would be heard over the racket. Fang was adding to the general chaos. "Better be damned important," he muttered as he slid the 9mm into the back waistband of his jeans.

Selena. What was she doing on his doorstep at this time of the night? Almost before he had the door open, his ex-wife was in his arms, bawling at the top of her lungs and babbling obscenities about Chandler. Crap—he didn't need this. Not right now.

"It's okay. Shh. It'll be fine." C.J. rubbed her back and made comforting noises. All the while he was trying to decide what Mom would do if he gutted his brother.

"Come on back to the kitchen. I'll get you a drink." He pushed Selena toward the kitchen and guided her into a chair. Fang jumped on her lap and did his usual kissy routine. The dog was a sucker for a good-looking woman.

"I have beer," he said, inventorying the contents of the refrigerator. "Shiner or Corona, and I also have wine." He held out a half-empty bottle for her inspection. "Afraid I don't have anything stronger." C.J. waited for an answer. Selena's tears had dried, but the occasional hiccup still popped through.

"Corona, please," she answered, wiping her face with the end of her T-shirt.

C.J. set the two beers on the table and took her hand. "Okay, what's the problem?"

She took a big gulp of Corona and hiccupped again. Fang took that as an invitation to sneak in a few more kisses. "It's Chandler. It's always Chandler—he's a lowlife, deplorable jerk! We had a horrible fight." She sniffed and blew her nose on a paper napkin. "We both said awful things that can't be taken back."

Her next sentence was muttered so softly C.J. couldn't hear her. "So what did you say?" he asked.

Selena raised her tearstained face. "I don't think he loves me."

Of all the things she could have said that was the most astonishing. Hot damn! Selena was in love with Chandler. And C.J. was positive the feeling was mutual. But forcing his obstinate sibling to admit it might require a good old knuckle sandwich.

"Tell you what." He took her half-finished beer and picked up Fang. "You can spend the night here." He patted her back, hoping to give some comfort. Crying women. There oughta be a manual. "We'll figure it out in the morning. Don't worry."

That should give him time to get Chandler's take on the situation. This was so reminiscent of their childhood, C.J. had to laugh. Their usual way of settling a dispute was a knock-down drag-out fight out in the backyard, so he'd talk to Chandler and *then* give him a pounding.

"I'm not ever going home, not with that man there," she proclaimed rather emphatically.

"Tell you what, why don't you take a nice bubble bath? It'll make you feel better." At least a soak in the tub always seemed to make Olivia very, *very* happy. And it would give him some time and privacy. He chucked Selena's chin and was rewarded by a watery smile. "I'll put your car in the garage and even get you another beer. Does that sound good?"

C.J. guided her into the bathroom and ran a tub

of sudsy water. "Did you bring any clothes?" he asked, although he hadn't seen a bag.

"No, I didn't think about anything but getting away."

"That's okay. I have some running shorts and a T-shirt."

C.J. returned with a set of clean clothes. "The towels are in the cabinet and the shampoo and other stuff is in there, too." Olivia had left some things—shampoo, lotion, girlie things. "Help yourself to anything you want. I'll be out in the garage."

"Hmm. Okay."

She didn't bother to ask what fascinating project he had going on in the garage. A good thing she wasn't curious. His conversation with Chandler would require privacy. That boy had a lot of explaining to do.

C.J.'S EXPLORER WAS in the driveway so he was at home—thank goodness! She hadn't been sure how long his meeting would last.

Olivia pulled the 'Vette behind the sheriff's car and retrieved the piggy bank. She resisted the urge to hold it in two fingers. It was repugnant, ugly and perhaps even dangerous, but it wasn't radioactive.

When Olivia knocked at the front screen, Fang was there to yap a welcome. She opened the door and bent over to scratch behind his ears. "How's my boy?" The dog rolled on his back, exposing his stomach for more attention. Of course, Olivia complied with some vigorous rubbing.

"C.J." she called, looking back over her shoulder

to the open door. That was odd—he didn't normally leave his house unlocked. The sound of music drifted from the back of the house, where the master bedroom and bath were located. C.J., bed, music. Hmm, that had potential. She tiptoed down the hall although stealth wasn't really necessary—the music was so loud a herd of elephants could have been marching by and he wouldn't have heard them.

The bathroom door wasn't quite closed, so when Olivia tapped with her finger, it slid open with a squeak.

She peeked around the sill and saw...

Selena! What was she doing in C.J.'s tub? For a moment Olivia had a flash of jealousy, but then she glanced at the ring on her finger. It was a promise of "forever after" and whatever the redhead was doing here had nothing to do with Olivia's relationship with C.J. He loved her and she loved him. Any remnant of jealousy was gone. She really, really trusted him and even more astonishing, she was ready to face her wedding phobia.

C.J. HAD RETREATED to the garage for his argument with Chandler. Talk about someone who had a commitment problem. The guy was world-class.

He had just punched in Chandler's cell number when he heard a car drive up. He peeked out the garage door and caught sight of Olivia's 'Vette. Great. Just fantastic. Selena was in his bathtub and Olivia had disappeared inside the house. Afraid he was going to have referee a catfight, C.J. raced in.

But he was either too late or a miracle had occurred. Olivia was leaning into the refrigerator retrieving a couple of Coronas.

"Let me take this to Selena and then I have something really important to tell you," she said before she strolled down the hall and disappeared into the master bedroom.

If the Gulf of Mexico had miraculously parted, he couldn't have been more surprised. Completely flummoxed, he got his own Corona and collapsed at the kitchen table. She wasn't jealous. Was that really Olivia or had the body snatchers made a visit to the Gulf Coast?

The question was answered when she returned to the kitchen and snuggled in his lap.

Yep—this was his girl. He didn't know why she was clutching a hideous pink piggy bank, and he didn't know why she was being so mellow about Selena, but this woman was definitely Olivia.

She prefaced her story with a hot, hot kiss—sometimes pleasure before business was good. "See this." Olivia held up the pig. "This atrocity is the key to the Super Saver fiasco, the break-ins, everything." She told him about Florene and Wilbur, the computer disk and Pit Viper.

"Hot damn." He'd suspected for some time the bikers and the Hardaways were connected, but this story was one for the books. It would give him great pleasure to round up the ersatz preacher and his wife. They had created havoc in his little corner of the world.

C.J. was busy indulging in a brief necking session when he heard a discreet cough. Selena! He came up for air and sure enough, there was Selena watching them with a big grin on her face.

"If you ladies will excuse me." He kissed Olivia again. "I have some bad guys to catch."

Chapter Thirty-Six

In addition to dealing with the flotsam and jetsam of everyday county crime, C.J. was working diligently to track down the Hardaways and Pit Viper's buddies. Just this morning, there had been a credible sighting of Florene and Wilbur (aka Yvonne and Mad Dog) near Dallas, heading north. He wasn't worried—they *would* be apprehended. Ditto for Pit Viper and his crew.

With everything happening so quickly, he hadn't had a chance to really talk to Olivia. She'd apparently mellowed about Selena, and that was good. However, he didn't understand how Olivia could say she loved him and still be so hesitant about setting a wedding date. Heck, she refused to even talk about moving in together.

The more he thought about it, the more convinced he became that it was showdown time. She had to make a real commitment. C.J. shut down his computer and informed the dispatcher he was leaving for the day.

"Come on, Fang, we're gonna have a nice talk with Olivia. It's time for her to fish or cut bait."

Fang danced around his feet, obviously overjoyed at the prospect of seeing his future mama.

OLIVIA WAS TRANSCRIBING patient notes when she heard a noise in the foyer. It was after business hours, so the staff was gone, and it was too early for the cleaning crew. With a bit of trepidation she peeked out her office door.

Good Lord! It was Brian. What was her ex-fiancé doing here? Her life had become one bizarre surprise after another.

"Brian. You're the last person in the world I expected to see," she said calmly. After the weird conversation they'd had last month, she'd managed to avoid at least a dozen other calls. But thank goodness, she hadn't actually seen the jerk since the night before their scheduled wedding. Even after he'd left her standing at the altar, the coward hadn't had the good manners to face her and explain his little disappearing act. He'd sent her a note. A note!

"You wouldn't take my calls, so I decided to come down."

Olivia studied her ex—tall, nice-looking and still sporting a smarmy smile. What a phony!

"I heard you're divorced."

He flashed her one of his patented grins. "So you've been keeping up with me."

Mother Mary! What had she seen in this guy? Oh, yeah, she'd been young, stupid, and naive. When they'd met in vet school, he'd seemed so sophisticated.

"I thought maybe we could go out to dinner and talk about old times."

That would be over her dead body.

"Seriously, Liv, we had something special, and I'd like to see if we still have that spark." He leaned forward as if to kiss her.

If he so much as put a paw on her, he'd live to regret it. Just the thought of kissing him made her want to gag.

He was invading her personal space, but Olivia really didn't think he'd do anything. However, she was big-time wrong. He grabbed her and was trying for a serious kiss.

Before she could react and clout the jerk, she heard the front door slam open. Uh-oh! That had to be C.J., and he wasn't going to be a happy camper.

C.J. COULDN'T BELIEVE his eyes. Who was the tall dude with his lips all over Olivia? Obviously he had a death wish.

"Olivia?" He was trying his best to remain calm.

"C.J." She pushed against the man's chest and spun toward C.J. "This is Brian."

"Brian?" Surely this couldn't be *the* Brian.

"It's not what you think," she said.

"And what do you think I think?" The woman he loved right down to the marrow of his bones was in the middle of a full-fledged lip lock with an ex-fiancé.

C.J. could tell he was about to lose his cool. He'd done everything a man could possibly do, short of standing on his head and whistling Dixie, and the woman was still busting his chops.

Olivia claimed she loved him, but she seemed incapable of making a commitment and without that commitment they were dead in the water. As much as it pained him to admit it, he was probably better off without her. At least a clean break would save his sanity—or maybe not. At the very least, he had to get out of there and do some thinking.

Oops! "C.J., listen to me." Olivia grabbed the front of his shirt, intent on making him understand. But then she looked into a pair of green eyes that were as stormy as a category four hurricane. The dimples were gone, the smile was missing, and the cocky charm was definitely absent. The man standing before her was a stranger—an angry stranger.

Olivia took a deep breath, a very deep breath, and tried to regroup. Rose always said that even a fish wouldn't get into trouble if it kept its mouth shut. Well, this time she felt like a great big flounder. This was an "oops" of monumental proportions, and it was all Brian's fault.

"Brian, get out of here and don't ever come back," she commanded, and he took off like the rat he was.

She was almost afraid to face C.J. She'd never seen him quite so upset. "Please listen to me. I didn't have anything to do with him coming here. And I certainly wasn't kissing him."

When he spoke it was so quiet, Olivia had to lean forward to hear him.

"You could've fooled me." He shook his head ruefully. "But we really have a bigger problem than Brian. You're not willing to make a commitment, and I love you too much not to have a 'till death do us part' promise. I don't think I can do it anymore." With those final words, he flipped his car keys in his hand and left.

Olivia tried to organize her thoughts, but the sound of the Explorer screeching out of the driveway was the only thing she could process. Aarrggh—a primal scream was itching to get out. Instead she issued a heartfelt one-word comment. "Crap!"

Olivia had waited too long to make a decision and now she was in a big mess of trouble. If she couldn't make this one right, her heart would suffer Humpty Dumpty's fate.

No doubt about it—she was the biggest moron in south Texas.

Chapter Thirty-Seven

After the debacle with Brian, Olivia halfway expected C.J. to cool down and call her, but he didn't. If the grapevine was accurate, he had talked to Rose, and Lolly, and Christian, and probably even the janitor—but he hadn't called her. And that was why she hijacked Lolly for lunch and advice.

"I'm miserable and I've been pigging out on comfort food," Olivia admitted. "But nothing's working." She poked a fork at the pile of mashed potatoes on her plate. "So maybe I'll just stop eating. At least I won't be dumped, miserable and *obese*."

"You are such a fool. He still loves you. We just have to come up with a plan."

"I've left C.J. so many messages I feel like a stalker. And after he changed his cell number, I started getting that new pizza place out on the highway. He changed his number. Can you believe that?" Olivia pounded her hand on the table and stabbed at her potatoes again. "So *what* is our plan?"

Lolly nibbled on her salad as she studied her friend.

"I know I'll rue the day we had this conversation, but I'll talk to Christian and see what he thinks. If anyone can get into C.J.'s brain, it's my husband."

"Oh God, would you really? I need help." It might take a miracle, but so be it. Olivia Alvarado wasn't about to let her man get away, even if she had to kidnap and hog-tie him until he forgave her.

Kidnap? Hmm.

"How many years do you get for the felony kidnapping of a law-enforcement officer? Hypothetically speaking, of course?"

Lolly choked on a piece of lettuce. "Not a good idea. We'll come up with another solution. But let me tell you, I can't believe some of the things *you* come up with. You're as crazy as he is."

"Regardless of the fact that he's not speaking to me right this minute, he *does* love me."

"I suspect you're right." Lolly didn't tell her friend that C.J. had been so grumpy everyone was avoiding him. Rumor had it his deputies had passed a hat to get him a one-way ticket to Siberia.

"TELL ME AGAIN why we're doing this?" Christian asked his wife as he stopped the van in front of the senior center.

Lolly had serious doubts about the viability of this scheme. But with the help of Rose, Mee Maw, Aunt Sissy, Corrine, Selena and Chandler—it seemed like everyone was tired of C.J.'s grumpy mood—they'd cooked up something that might or might not work. At best, it was still dim-witted.

"Because they're morons and we have to help them." Lolly responded. "They've been so busy running from each other, they don't know when to quit. And *your* friend is as stubborn as a Missouri mule."

"He's your friend, too."

"Yeah, and *my* friend Olivia is no lightweight in the stubborn category."

"Just for the record, I think this is stupid."

"Yeah. I do, too. But we couldn't come up with anything else that would get him here."

C.J. WAS KNEE-DEEP in paperwork when the desk sergeant stuck his head in the door. "Hey, boss, you have a call on line two. She won't take no for an answer."

C.J. looked up from the file he was reading. "Who is it and what does she want?"

The dispatcher had the audacity to chuckle. "It's Marcela Hamilton. She said to tell you they're about to have a riot at the senior center. It's over a bingo game."

The man had the audacity to chuckle all the way back to his desk. So much for paperwork!

"Hey, Miz Hamilton, what's up?" The racket he could hear in the background didn't bode well for a telephone solution to the problem.

"Hi, C.J. Well, it's like this. Sissy and I decided to go to the senior center for bingo. They're giving away a plasma TV, you know, one of those big flat ones."

"Yes, ma'am." *Now finish the rest of the story.*

"Anyway, when we got here, we found out that

Buddy Holidecker is the caller, and everyone knows he's deaf as a post."

The background noise grew louder. "Yes, ma'am." C.J. reached for his Stetson. This would definitely require a visit.

"Anyway, he kept calling numbers after Mrs. Pomerantz got a bingo and you can only imagine what happened after that. Gladys Schmidt got involved in the fracas."

Yep, this demanded his personal attention. "I'll be over in ten minutes. Can you keep the ladies from assaulting someone till I get there?"

With Marcela's assurance ringing in his ears, he whistled for Fang. "Let's go, buddy. We have ladies to calm down."

"DID IT WORK? Is he coming?" Lolly asked her mother. If anything would get him there, it would be something involving Mrs. Pomerantz. But as with all good conspiracies, nothing was a certainty.

"He's coming." Marcela did a high-five with Mrs. P. Veteran matchmakers, the seniors had dived into the plot headfirst. Olivia was the only person in the hall who looked less than enthusiastic.

"I'm having my doubts about this." She shrugged. "What if he still won't talk to me?"

Aunt Sissy patted her hand. "He's a man. Once he gets a gander at you, he won't be thinking about talking. Kissing is a much better form of communication."

"Is everyone ready? We want lots of noise when he pulls up." Lolly instructed. "And Buddy—" The bingo caller failed to respond. "Buddy!" she screamed. "You have to pretend to be in a rumble with Mrs. P."

"Okay," he bellowed.

C.J.'s BS METER WAS on high alert. He spied Olivia's 'Vette hidden next door and Lolly's minivan parked down the street. What were those two up to? He left the Explorer by the front door and stalked in.

It wasn't until he caught a flash of red hair—a sight that was so out of context in the sea of gray— that he was absolutely positive he'd been conned. Hail, hail, the gang was all there—Chandler, Selena, Rose, Raul, Lolly, Christian and Olivia. Yep, they'd pulled off a sting.

Ignoring Olivia and her friends, he strolled over to Marcela and Sissy. "What's going on?"

Before he could get an answer, Mrs. P. joined them.

UH-OH! This was playing out exactly as Olivia was afraid it would. He was still mad. "This was such a dumb plan," she wailed. "He acted like he didn't even see me." She twisted the engagement ring on her left hand.

"Just wait. We haven't played our trump card yet," Lolly said. "I'm sure it'll work, even if Mama and Aunt Sissy did dream it up. Good God, those two are devious."

Fang sidled up to Olivia waiting to be cuddled. "Hi, sweetie," she said as she picked him up and rubbed his ears.

"See what's happening up there?" Lolly pointed

at the conference involving C.J., Mrs. Pomerantz and Buddy Holidecker.

"And check out C.J.'s grin. It's gonna work."

Pray God she was right, because if this one went south, Olivia was fresh out of ideas. However, the thought of leaving her fate in the hands of Mee Maw and Aunt Sissy, the ditzy sisters, didn't give her a great deal of confidence.

"Ladies and gentlemen, we're going to have a bingo game in honor of our sheriff." Someone without the need of a hearing aid had taken over from Buddy Holidecker. "So grab your cards and get ready to play. The bingo will be to cover your entire card and the prize is three dozen homemade tamales from Gutierrez Taqueria. Just thinkin' about those tamales makes my mouth water. So get ready to bingo."

C.J. recognized a setup when saw it, but he played along waiting to see what would happen. His curiosity was killing him. Olivia *had* to love him, or she wouldn't have gone to this much trouble. Yes sir, she loved him. Praise the Lord! But he wasn't about to make it easy for her. So he continued to ignore the woman he loved and sat down to play bingo with Mrs. Pomerantz and Gladys Schmidt.

"You know, ladies, you'd make my job a whole lot easier if you took up knitting."

"Who says you can't get into trouble knittin'?" Gladys giggled as she marked the first number on her card.

Throughout an interminable bingo game, C.J. managed, through sheer determination, not to glance in Olivia's direction. Or at least not until the caller announced B-19 and a very familiar and feminine voice in the corner called "Bingo." He glanced down at his card and realized he was also a winner. This amazing coincidence had to be karma, or the work of the most devious bunch of seniors in the Lone Star state—and he was betting on the latter. Half the people in the hall had probably bingoed thirty minutes ago.

C.J. strolled over to Olivia and held up his card with all the numbers marked out. "Guess we're going to have to share those tamales." He was pleased to notice she didn't seem at all comfortable with the situation. "Or, Livy darlin', you can have them all to yourself if you'll give me a kiss." Before she could answer, he brought her to her feet.

And what a kiss it was! Delicious, delightful, delectable. He was leaving a trail of kisses from her earlobe to the corner of her mouth, down to her neck, and back up again. If only he'd keep it up for the next century. Fang skittered around their feet wanting to get in on the action.

C.J. pulled away and rested his forehead against hers. "Oh, Livy. I had to do that. I've been going out of my mind for the past two weeks."

"You're not mad at me?" she asked hopefully, pretty sure the word *mad* was not in his current vocabulary.

"Uh-uh. Here's the deal. I trust you, and I love you so much it makes me crazy." He lifted her hand and kissed the finger that still held his ring. "And I know you love me. But we have to have a mutual trust of each other. We can't have a life together if there isn't trust. And I'm not willing to settle for anything less than marriage."

"I trust you," she whispered. "I trust you with my life, my love, everything. And if you want to get married this afternoon, I'm ready."

"Really?"

He had a right to be suspicious, but this was the most important conversation they'd ever had.

"Really." She couldn't resist a little nibble on his neck. "I had things all messed up in my mind, but now I have my head on straight. You're my soul mate. I thought I lost you and I didn't think I'd survive that."

His dimple had made a sudden appearance. "So you'll trust me even if I stay out all night drinking with the boys?"

Olivia suppressed a wince, even though she was fairly sure he was kidding. "Even then. Yeah, even then," she repeated, her tone a bit more sure the second time.

It began as a chuckle and ended as a full-blown belly laugh. "Damn, I'm a lucky man. Did I ever tell you I love you?" C.J. kissed her once, took a deep breath and started all over, then pulled back and cleared his throat.

"I think we have an audience."

Ye gads! She'd almost forgotten where they were. The applause started as a ripple and grew to a Friday night football decibel.

"It looks like they approve." C.J. underlined that comment with another kiss. "Did you see what I saw?" he asked when he came up for air.

"What?" The crazy man was asking questions when she was having a hard time remembering her own name.

"Selena and Chandler were over in the corner necking."

"Hot dog. Love must be in the air." Olivia turned to their audience. "You're all invited to a wedding. Date and time to be announced, but it'll be soon. Very, very soon!"

Fang plopped down on C.J.'s boot and gave a Great Dane–sized burp.

"Okay, who's been feeding this dog?" C.J. and Olivia exclaimed in unison.

* * * * *

*In Ann DeFee's next American Romance,
Mee Maw and Sissy take off on that
road trip to discover the highways and
byways of Texas—
and to meet some good-looking
men who actually remember Elvis
in his prime.*
**Watch for SOMEWHERE DOWN IN TEXAS,
coming in March 2007!**